The Vineyards of Calanetti
Saying "I do" under the Tuscan sun...

Deep in the Tuscan countryside nestles the picturesque village of Monte Calanetti. Famed for its world-renowned vineyards, the village is also home to the crumbling but beautiful Palazzo di Comparino. Empty for months, rumors of a new owner are spreading like wildfire...and that's before the village is chosen as the setting for the royal wedding of the year!

It's going to be a roller coaster of a year, but will wedding bells ring out in Monte Calanetti for anyone else?

Find out in this fabulously heartwarming, uplifting and thrillingly romantic new eight-book continuity from Harlequin Romance!

A Bride for the Italian Boss by Susan Meier

Return of the Italian Tycoon by Jennifer Faye

Reunited by a Baby Secret by Michelle Douglas

Soldier, Hero...Husband? by Cara Colter

His Lost-and-Found Bride by Scarlet Wilson

The Best Man & the Wedding Planner
by Teresa Carpenter

His Princess of Convenience by Rebecca Winters

Saved by the CEO by Barbara Wallace

Dear Reader,

Welcome back to Monte Calanetti!

At last, we learn why Louisa Harrison has come to Tuscany. Turns out the palazzo owner has been hiding a couple secrets—secrets that have landed her back in the tabloids. Fortunately for her, vineyard owner Nico Amatucci is around to help protect her from the paparazzi. *Un*fortunately for her, Nico is everything that she's vowed to stay away from.

Or is he? Once she starts peeling back the layers, Louisa learns there's a lot more to the vintner than a sexy smile and a need to take charge. Behind the good looks beats the heart of a man scarred by a chaotic childhood.

As for Nico...well, he's about to discover what it's like to fall in love for the very first time.

I like to tell people that their romance unfolds during harvest season when the grapes (and happy endings) are at their sweetest.

Writing this letter is a little bittersweet because it means The Vineyards of Calanetti series has come to an end. I was honored when Harlequin asked me to be part of this fantastic series as there were so many wonderful authors involved: Susan Meier, Jennifer Faye, Michelle Douglas, Scarlet Wilson, Cara Colter, Teresa Carpenter and Rebecca Winters. Each of them brought their own special vision to Monte Calanetti, and the result is an eight-book series as rich as any Italian wine. (How's that for a metaphor?) If you haven't read their Calanetti books yet, you're missing out!

As always, thanks for reading.

Barbara

Saved by the CEO

Barbara Wallace

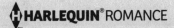

HARLEQUIN® ROMANCE

Recycling programs for this product may not exist in your area.

Special thanks and acknowledgment are given to Barbara Wallace for her contribution to The Vineyards of Calanetti series.

ISBN-13: 978-0-373-74372-8

Saved by the CEO

First North American Publication 2016

Copyright © 2016 by Harlequin Books S.A.

www.Harlequin.com

Printed in U.S.A.

Barbara Wallace can't remember when she wasn't dreaming up love stories in her head, so writing romances for Harlequin Romance is a dream come true. Happily married to her own Prince Charming, she lives in New England with a house full of empty-nest animals. Occasionally her son comes home, as well.

To stay up-to-date on Barbara's news and releases, sign up for her newsletter at barbarawallace.com.

Books by Barbara Wallace

Harlequin Romance

In Love with the Boss

A Millionaire for Cinderella
Beauty & Her Billionaire Boss

Daring to Date the Boss
Mr. Right, Next Door!
The Courage to Say Yes
The Man Behind the Mask
The Unexpected Honeymoon

Visit the Author Profile page
at Harlequin.com for more titles.

To my fellow Calanetti creators for making this project so fun to work on.
And to Carol, Val, Darlene and Michelle, who always make me feel like a rock star.
Thanks.

CHAPTER ONE

"I THINK I'M in love."

Louisa Harrison bit off a piece of *cornetto*, moaning as the sweet cake-like pastry melted like butter on her tongue. Crumbs dotted her chin. She caught them with her finger, not wanting to waste a drop. "Seriously, Dani, how do you not weigh a thousand pounds living with this man?" If she were married to a chef as wonderful as Rafe Mancini, she'd be the size of her palazzo, the grounds and the vineyards combined.

Her best friend laughed. "Trust me, it's not easy. Fortunately, running around the restaurant all day keeps me in shape. Especially now. Ever since the royal wedding, we've been slammed with requests for reservations. Everyone wants to eat at the restaurant that fed Prince Antonio and his bride."

"As well they should." Danielle's husband, Rafe, entered the restaurant dining room brandishing a coffeepot. "You make it sound as though Mancini's is some ordinary royal wedding caterer."

"I'm not sure there is such a thing as an *ordinary* royal wedding caterer," Dani replied, kissing him on the cheek, "but you're right, Mancini's is anything but ordinary. Once people taste Rafe's food, they are desperate to come back."

"Only they can't for at least eight weeks. My beautiful bride is right—we are booked solid through the harvest festival."

"That's fantastic," Louisa replied helping herself to a cup of coffee. Rafe Mancini not only created wonderful food, he made the best American coffee in Tuscany. That was Dani's doing. She'd insisted Rafe add a few New World touches to his traditionally Italian menu to placate US tourists. One of many small changes she'd implemented over the past few months. It hadn't taken long for her friend to establish herself as an equal partner both in the relationship and the business. But then, Louisa had heard there were men in this world who actually liked when their wives had minds of their own. Not to mention lives.

She just hadn't married one.

"Mancini's isn't the only place that's doing well," Dani continued. "Business has been up all around the village. Donatella told me sales at the boutique are up over 40 percent from last year."

Louisa wasn't surprised. Over the past nine months, Monte Calanetti had gone from sleepy

Tuscan village to must-see tourist destination. Not only had they been selected to host Halencia's royal wedding—considered the wedding of the year in most circles—but art experts had recently discovered an unknown fresco masterpiece hidden in the local chapel. Now it felt as if every person in Italy, tourist or resident, made a point of driving through the town. That they arrived to discover a picture-perfect village *and* an Italian *Good Food* rated restaurant owned by one of Europe's premier chefs only enhanced the town's allure.

"Quite a change from when you and I arrived here, huh?" she noted. It'd been an early spring day when the two of them had met on the bus from Florence. Two expatriates, each on her own quest to the Tuscan Valley. For Dani, the tiny village represented a last adventure before deciding on her future. Louisa, on the other hand, had taken one look at the terracotta roofs rising from the valley and decided luck had granted her the perfect place to escape her past. A place where she could heal.

"I knew as soon as I stepped off the bus that Monte Calanetti was special," Dani said. "There's something magical about this town. You can feel it."

More like her friend felt the attraction between her and the man she eventually married; there'd been sparks from the second Dani and Rafe had laid eyes on each other. Louisa kept the thought to herself. "The royal wedding planner certainly thought so," she said instead.

"Unfortunately, we can't ride the wedding momentum forever. Once harvest season ends, people will be more interested in the ski resorts." Rafe said.

"People will still seek out Mancini's," Louisa said.

"Some, yes, but certainly not the numbers we've been enjoying. And they certainly won't spend time visiting other businesses."

True. So much of Monte Calanetti's appeal revolved around being able to stroll its cobblestone streets during the warm weather. It would be hard to make a wish in the plaza fountain if the water was frozen. There was a part of Louisa that wouldn't mind the crowds thinning. She missed the early days when she could walk the streets without worrying that some American tourist would recognize her. Another part, however—the practical part— knew the village needed more than a seasonal income. Prior to the wedding, several of the smaller businesses had been on shaky ground.

A third part reminded her she needed income, too. Till now she'd been surviving on the money the royal family had paid her to use her property, and that was almost gone.

"It won't matter if Mancini's is the best restaurant in the world, if it's surrounded by empty buildings,"

Rafe was saying. "We need something that will encourage people to spend time here year-round."

Funny he should say that. Louisa sipped her coffee thoughtfully. The practical part of her had also been kicking around an idea lately. It was only a germ at the moment, but it might help the cause. "It would be nice to see the village continue to prosper," she had to admit. Even though she, like Dani, was a relative newcomer, she'd already come to consider the place home, and nobody wanted to see their home suffer economically.

"What do you have in mind?" she asked him. He obviously had something up his sleeve or he wouldn't have put on this breakfast.

Pushing up his sleeves, the chef rested his forearms against the edge of the table and leaned close. "I was thinking we could start some kind of committee."

"Like a chamber of commerce?" Did they even have those in Italy? They must.

"Nothing so formal. I'm picturing local business leaders brainstorming ideas like the harvest festival that we can put on to attract traffic."

"And since the palazzo is such a big part of the village..." Dani started.

"You'd like me to be on the committee." That made sense, especially if she carried through with her own idea. "Count me in... What?"

Her friend and her husband had suddenly become

very interested in their breakfast plates. "There's one problem," Dani said.

"Problem?" Louisa's fingers gripped her fork. "What kind of problem?" As if she didn't know what the problem would be. Question was, how had they found out?

"I want Nico Amatucci on the committee, as well," Rafe answered bluntly.

Oh. Her fear vanished in a rush, replaced by a completely different type of tension. One that started low in her stomach and moved in waves through her. "Why would that be a problem?"

"Well," Dani said, "we know the two of you haven't always gotten along…"

Memories of wine-tinged kisses flashed to life. "That's in the past," she replied. "We worked together on cleaning up the plaza, remember?"

"I know, but…"

"But what?"

The couple exchanged a look. "At the wedding, you two looked like you'd had a falling-out."

Louisa would have called it a momentary loss of her senses. "It's no big deal." And it wasn't. Beneath the table, her fingers tapped out a rhythm on her thigh. In comparison to what she thought they were going to say, her "falling-out" with Nico amounted to nothing.

She barely remembered, she thought, tongue running over her lower lip.

"Working together won't be awkward, then?" Rafe asked.

"Don't be silly—Nico and I are adults. I'm sure we can handle sitting on a committee together."

"What committee?"

As if waiting for his cue, Nico Amatucci strolled into the dining room. If he were someone else, Louisa would accuse him of waiting to make a dramatic entrance, but in his case dramatic entrances came naturally.

"Sorry I'm late," he said. "We've been working around the clock since the wedding. It appears people can't get enough of Amatucci Red." The last part was said looking straight at her. As Louisa met his gaze, she forced herself to keep as cool an expression as possible and prayed he couldn't see how fast her heart was racing. This was the first time she'd seen him since the wedding. The vintner looked as gorgeous as ever.

He'd come straight from the fields. The ring of dampness around his collar signaled hours of hard work, as did the dirt streaking his jeans and T-shirt. Louisa spied a couple smudges on his neck, too, left behind after wiping the sweat from his skin. She'd say this about the man: he worked as hard as his employees. Something he, as the owner of one of Tuscany's finest boutique wineries, didn't have to do. Probably did it to make up for the fact he was arrogant and presumptuous.

A frown marred his Romanesque features as he pointed to the coffeepot. "American?"

"That a problem?" Rafe asked.

"No." His sigh was long and exaggerated.

Rafe rolled his eyes. "There's no need to be dramatic. If you want espresso, just say so."

"Make it a double," Nico called after him with a grin. "I've been up since sunrise."

Despite there being three empty seats on the other side of the table, he chose to sit in the one his friend had just vacated, which positioned him directly next to Louisa. "I trust I didn't keep you waiting too long," he said to her. His crooked smile made the comment sound more like a dirty secret. But then, that's what Nico Amatucci did. He used his charm to lure people into bending to his will. When they didn't bend to his authority, that is. His sensual mouth and sparkling dark eyes could worm their way past a person's defenses, trapping them in his spell before they knew what was happening.

He reached for a *cornetto*, his shoulder brushing against Louisa's as he moved. The hours of hard work had left him smelling of fresh-tilled dirt and exertion. It was a primal, masculine scent, and though Louisa tried her best not to react, her own basic instincts betrayed her and she shivered anyway. To cover, she ignored his question and took a long sip of coffee.

Nico countered by taking a bite of pastry. "Has everyone recovered from the wedding?" he asked, licking the crumbs off his thumb. Louisa narrowed her eyes. She swore he was purposely trying to make the action erotic. Especially when he added, "I know I'm still feeling the aftereffects. Are you?"

Again, he looked straight at her. Louisa lifted her chin. "Not at all," she replied with a crispness that made her proud.

Apparently it wasn't crisp enough, since he reacted with little more than an arched brow. "Are you sure?"

Dani jumped to her feet. "I'm going to go see if Rafe needs help. Marcello rearranged the pantry yesterday, and you know how he gets when he can't find things."

Who did she think she was fooling? Rafe wouldn't allow anyone to rearrange his pantry without supervision.

"Subtle," Nico remarked when Dani was out of earshot. "One would think she was trying to give us time alone."

"One would think," Louisa muttered in return. "Though I don't know why."

"Perhaps she thinks we need to talk."

"Well, she would be wrong. We don't need to talk about anything."

"I see. Is that why you're avoiding me, *bella mia*?"

His beauty indeed. *I'm not your anything*, she wanted to snap. She didn't belong to anyone. Not anymore. And especially not to someone like him. Bad enough she let herself fall under his spell at the wedding. "Who says I've been avoiding anyone? Maybe I've been busy. You're not the only one who's had a lot to do since the wedding."

"My apologies. You're right." His chair made a scratching noise on the floor as he angled it so they were facing one another. Taking the last *cornetto* from the center of the table, he tore the pastry in two and divided the pieces between their plates. "So tell me, what have you been up to that has kept you so busy?"

Louisa glared at the fluffy delicacy in front of her. "Things," she replied.

"Things?" His chuckle was smooth like syrup. "That's a very broad category."

"I'm a very broad person."

"Ah, *bella mia.* 'Broad' is definitely not what I would call you." His hand moved forward. Thinking he was about to brush the bangs from her eyes, Louisa jerked back, only to turn red when he picked up his half of the pastry. "I wanted to talk about what happened at the wedding."

"I told you, there's nothing to talk about. We made a mistake, that's all. Why don't we forget it ever happened?"

Sounds from the kitchen drifted into the restaurant as Nico chewed his pastry. Louisa listened, trying to determine how far away she was from rescue. There was an uneasy familiarity to the way they sat with Nico's leg close but not touching hers.

Slowly his eyes lifted to meet hers. "What if I don't want to forget?"

"One double espresso as ordered!" Rafe announced. The chef returned to the dining room carrying a gold-rimmed demitasse. Behind him trailed Dani, who shot Nico a look. From their mutually taut expressions, Louisa wondered if there hadn't been a disagreement over interrupting the conversation. She offered a silent thank-you to whichever one of them had won.

First thing Dani did when she sat down was to try to catch Louisa's eye, but Louisa continued to stare at the tablecloth and prayed that the floor might swallow her up. She hated scrutiny. Hated the feel of people's eyes upon her. Trying to look inside her. Thinking they could read her thoughts. Her fingers crept to her neckline to tug the suddenly too-tight collar.

"Will there be anything else, your highness?" Thank God for Rafe. Again. He set the cup on the table with a flourish, forcing Nico's attention back to the business at hand.

The vintner's bronze fingers wrapped around the handle. "This will do for now," he replied.

"You do know that when I said 'your highness,' I meant it sarcastically, right?"

"Yes, but you wait on me all the same." Nevertheless, Nico saluted his friend with the cup before taking a sip. "So," he said after he swallowed, "you said something about a committee?"

"You *were* listening," Rafe replied. "Yes, I want to create a committee for developing tourism."

"Monte Calanetti already has a person in charge of tourism." Nico explained. "Vincenzo Alberti."

"Tell me you're joking. Everyone knows Vincenzo did nothing and that the only reason we hosted the wedding was because your brother was in town to write the proposal. It could have just as easily gone to some place in Umbria."

"True. Vincenzo is rather useless."

"What I'm talking about is something independent and more grassroots. I'm certain if the local businesspeople put their heads together, we can come up with a host of ideas to increase tourism. Not to mention run them better."

"I certainly won't complain about increased business, especially during the dormant months," Nico said. Leaning back, he hooked an arm over the back of his chair. "Who else do you have in mind besides the four of us? I assume it is the four of us, since we're all sitting here."

The two men began tossing names back and forth,

some of whom Louisa recognized, some she didn't. She wasn't surprised when, as the conversation progressed, the dynamic between the friends shifted with Nico slowly taking the reins. That was something else Nico Amatucci did. No matter how commanding others might be—and Rafe certainly qualified as commanding—Nico was always the one in charge.

Her ex-husband had been the exact same way. Minus the rugged sensuality that is. Steven had been painstakingly glossy, his looks created from the pages of fashion magazines whereas Nico was more earthy. The kind of man who got his hands dirty from actually working with them, not from helping himself.

She remembered the roughness of Nico's calloused hands as his thumbs had fanned her cheeks…

And how effortlessly he'd managed to dance her into a secluded corner without her realizing. In charge till the end, just like Steven.

"We need to make it clear to everyone involved that we don't want to be too commercial," she heard him say. "It's one thing to increase tourism, it's another to lose the very thing that makes Monte Calanetti special."

Rafe agreed. "Absolutely. Ideally, we want events or attractions that highlight our traditions and Old World charm. That's what the tourists want. Maybe there's something we can do around the *Madonna and Child* painting in the chapel. Something historical."

"I read the other day that Santo Majorca is building a spa around its underground springs. Too bad we can't unearth a spring here."

"Wouldn't that be nice?"

"Ow!" Louisa jumped as pain shot up from her shin. Damn it, but Dani wore pointy shoes. That kick would leave a bruise.

The two men turned to look at her. "Everything all right?" Nico asked.

"Fine," she said, rubbing her leg. Beneath her index finger she could feel a small divot. There was definitely going to be a bruise.

Across the table, her friend didn't even have the decency to look apologetic. She was too busy gesturing with her eyebrows for Louisa to say something. Louisa replied with a shake of her head.

Why not? Dani mouthed.

Because of a zillion reasons. The concept was still too vague and unformed, for one. She wasn't ready for people to start poking holes in her idea. Or take it over, she thought, sliding a look in Nico's direction. She wasn't sure she was ready period.

"Did I miss something?" Nico asked.

Of course he would say something. Those sharp brown eyes didn't miss a thing, not that either she or Dani were being very subtle.

"Louisa's been working on a terrific idea," Dani said.

"Really?" He turned to face her. "What is it? If it's something that will help, by all means tell us."

"It's still at the very beginning stages. I haven't worked out all the details yet."

"But the general idea is brilliant. She wants to turn the palazzo into a hotel."

Some of Nico's enthusiasm faded in favor of concern. "What kind of hotel? You're not planning to alter the property, are you?"

"Nothing drastic, I assure you," she said as she shot a narrow-eyed look in Dani's direction. Why couldn't she have found an unenthusiastic best friend? "I was thinking of something more like a high-end boutique hotel."

"Isn't that a great idea?" Dani piped in, clearly unfazed by Louisa's glare. "People love to stay in historic buildings. Remember that couple last month who told us they were staying at Palazzo St. Rosa? They couldn't stop raving about the place."

"She's right, they couldn't," Rafe said. "No matter how hard I tried to make them."

"They showed us the photos, and the place can't hold a candle to Louisa's."

"That's because Palazzo di Comparino is special." Intended as both a compliment and a warning, Nico's comment made Louisa bristle. It'd been nine months since she'd moved in and he still acted as though the palazzo was his responsibility. And

Dani wondered why she didn't want to talk about her plans.

"Special, yes," she replied, "but it's also very large and expensive for one person to keep up." Especially if said person had no other source of income. "Opening it to the public is one way to cover some of the expenses." As well as help her stay independent. Being in charge, having total control of her life again, seemed almost too good to be true.

Maybe she could finally put the past behind her.

No sooner did the thought form than her old friend insecurity came rushing in to take its place. "Of course, the building needs a lot more upgrading before I can do much of anything, and I still have to secure financing. Who knows how long it'll take before anything happens."

"Well, I agree with Dani—I like the idea. A high-end hotel is exactly what Monte Calanetti needs," Rafe said as he warmed both her and Dani's coffee. "If you need anything, let us know. Nico and I will be glad to help. Isn't that right, Nico?"

"Absolutely." The vineyard owner slid his empty cup across the table for a refill, which Rafe immediately provided, remembering Nico preferred espresso. There was a roguish gleam in his eyes as he smiled. "As the two of us have proven, we make a good team, do we not?"

A good team. In a flash, Louisa's mind traveled back in time…

The Royal Wedding

"Ask and you shall receive. Your cake, *signorina*." Nico's exaggerated bow as he handed her a slice of cake made Louisa laugh. The wedding had brought out the lightheartedness in everyone, even her. It felt good, laughing. She'd faked happiness for so long that she was afraid she'd forgotten how to truly enjoy herself.

"Grazie," she replied with her best regal nod before noticing he'd returned with only one plate. "No slice for you? Don't tell me there isn't enough." She saw the cake; it was large enough to feed all of Italy.

"Ah, but it's more fun to share, don't you think?" From his breast pocket, he produced two forks. "To commemorate our successful partnership. We make a good team, do we not?"

"Surprisingly, yes." If anyone had told her that one day she and the vineyard owner would be civil to one another, let alone work together, she would have told them they were crazy. But the two of them had organized the massive village cleanup in preparation for today's wedding. As a result, the palazzo and the plaza had never looked lovelier—a pretty big achievement considering the village had started out picture-perfect.

And now, here they were enjoying each other's company at the wedding reception, as well. Things between them had definitely thawed since Louisa's first day in town when he'd demanded to see her ownership papers. Or maybe she was the one who was starting to thaw?

It certainly felt as though something inside her was shifting.

She focused her attention to the cake Nico was sliding toward her.

"If we're toasting, shouldn't we be raising a glass?" she asked, taking one of the forks.

"We've been raising our glasses all day. I thought we could use a change of pace." He moved his chair so that they were sitting side by side, close enough that his elbow nudged hers. Cutting off a bite of cake, he raised it in the air like a glass. "To teamwork."

"To teamwork."

Louisa moved to cut her own piece of cake, intending to salute him back, only to have him press the cake to her lips before she could. "The lady should always have the first bite," he said, his low voice.

A warm tightness moved through her as the fork slid between her teeth. Chocolate and raspberry melted on her tongue.

"Good?" he asked.

"Amazing." She ran a tongue over her lower lip, chasing the hint of frosting that had been left behind. "Try some."

With what could only be called a wicked smile, he

did, and when the fork disappeared into his mouth, the tightness in her stomach intensified. A hint of chocolate remained on her lips. Though tempted to lick the taste away, she reached for her napkin instead. After that display, running her tongue over her lips seemed too much like answering in kind and the summer air already felt thick and stifling.

While she'd never let him know it, Nico was quite possibly the most handsome man here, even more handsome than the crown prince. Months of working outdoors had left him with a permanent tan that gave everything else about him—his smile, his eyes, his crisp white shirt—a kind of brilliance the other men couldn't match.

Why on earth was he sitting here eating cake with her? Giving voice to her thoughts, she said, "I have to admit, I was surprised when you suggested we attend together." Handsome, rich…she assumed he had a black book of supermodels at the ready for occasions like this.

"Made sense, did it not? We're both here because our businesses are involved in the celebration.

"Why?" he asked with another grin. "Is there someone you would rather be sitting with?"

"Well, the best man is sort of attractive."

"The best man is only interested in the wedding planner. Face it, *bella mia*," he said, stretching an arm across the back of her chair. "I am the best offer you have."

Another laugh bubbled its way from her chest. She must have had too much wine because his arrogance was sounding damn sexy at the moment.

The room grew quiet. "*Signore e signori*, his Royal Highness Prince Antonio and his bride invite you to join them in this, their final dance of the evening."

"Wow," she said, "last dance already? Time goes by fast."

"Looks like my company was good after all."

Louisa cut another bite off the cake. "Don't get too carried away."

"Come on, admit it." He nudged her shoulder. "You had a good time."

"Yeah, I did." And for the first time in years, she meant it. This had been her first black-tie event since the divorce, and she'd feared the memories of her old life would prove too much to deal with, but Nico had proved a wonderfully entertaining companion. She was actually sorry to see the evening end.

"We need to dance," Nico said, setting down his fork in a way that made it sound more like a command. "One doesn't refuse an invitation from a future king."

Apparently not. All around the room, couples were making their way to the dance floor to join Antonio and his bride, Christina. A few feet away Dani and Rafe were already wrapped in each other's arms, as were Nico's brother, Angelo, and his fiancée. Even Nico's extremely pregnant sister, Marianna, was swaying to the music.

She looked back at the hand Nico was holding out. Such strong capable hands, she thought, the tightness giving way to an internal shiver. "I haven't danced in a long time," she warned. "Your feet might want to be prepared."

"Consider them forewarned."

She needn't have worried. As soon as Nico's arm entwined her waist, she forgot all about being rusty. Their bodies moved together like two synchronized pieces of a whole.

Nico's eyes swept the length of her. "I've been meaning to tell you how beautiful you look. You outshine the princess."

"Careful, talking like that could be considered treason in Halencia." She tried to brush off the compliment with a smile. Flattery had lost its meaning to her a long time ago. Looking good had been part of the requirements when she was married. Looking good, behaving properly, doing what she was told…all part of the job.

"I'll take the risk," he said as he pulled her close. Louisa's eyes locked with his as they moved across the floor. They were darker than she'd ever seen them, the pupils giant pools of black. While Steven always expected her to look beautiful, he never looked at her with such blatant appreciation. The glint in Nico's eyes made her feel like a bite of wedding cake, waiting to be sampled. The thought should have frightened her. Instead, hot shivers danced along her spine.

God, but it'd been a long time since she'd felt like a woman instead of a possession.

The orchestra faded away, drowned out by the sound of their breathing and the rasp of his jacket as it brushed her sequined bodice with every rise and fall of his chest.

She wasn't sure who leaned in first. Once his mouth closed over hers, who had made the first move didn't matter, not when his lips were moving against hers as if he were trying to kiss his way inside. She kissed him back just as hungrily, too many passionless years making her desperate. They kissed hard and deep, only stopping when the need to breathe became too much.

Blinking, Louisa slowly remembered where they were. "I—"

"Shh…" He pressed a kiss to the corner of her mouth. "It's okay, *bella mia*."

Bella mia. My lovely. *Mine*. Louisa stiffened.

"Don't worry," he said, misreading the reaction for embarrassment. "No one can see us."

Turning, she saw that they were in a secluded corner, just outside the ballroom door. While she'd been lost in his spell, Nico had steered them safely away from prying eyes.

How thoughtful and practiced of him. But then, men like Nico didn't do anything spontaneously, did they? They were always in control. Like hunters stalking prey, only instead of bullets they used smiles and seduction. Their victims were trapped in their gilded cages before they ever knew what was happening.

Except Louisa did know. And she was never ever going to be trapped again.

Pushing just enough so as to not make a scene, she stepped out of his embrace. "The bride and groom will be leaving shortly. I better make sure everything is set for their departure." She left him standing in the corner without turning back…

"Louisa?"

Yanked from the memory by the sound of Dani's voice, she saw the three of them staring at her. "You okay?" her friend asked.

"I'm fine," she lied. Part of her was still back on the dance floor, lost in a pair of dark eyes. "You were saying?"

"I was saying that as far as financing your hotel is concerned, I would consider investing…"

"No." She didn't mean for the word to come out so strongly, but Nico was looking straight at her while he spoke and the memory of how those eyes distracted her was so fresh…

Just as well, though. Better to be blunt than let

him think he had a chance. As an investor or anything else.

Monte Calanetti was her chance at a new life. No way was she going to let someone sweep in and mess things up.

Not this time.

CHAPTER TWO

Nico squinted and double-checked the line on the refractometer. "Twenty-two point four."

"Is that on schedule?"

"Close." Pulling the battered leather journal from his back pocket, he flipped through the pages until he found last year's data. "One hundredth of a point off," he reported before turning the page and making note of today's measurement. Even better than he expected. He'd been afraid the easy summer had accelerated the ripening process. So far, however, the sugar levels were holding close to previous years, which boded well for this year's vintage.

"When will you harvest?"

He turned to the young man at his elbow. Mario, a viticulture student from the university was hanging on his every word. "Depends upon the weather and the variety, but for Amatucci Red, I like the Brix level to be between twenty-five and twenty-six. A hair shy of precocious, as it were," he added with a chuckle.

Mario nodded as he took notes. Nico would never admit it out loud but he enjoyed being seen as a master. It made him feel as though he'd achieved what Carlos had hoped for him. "Precocious?" he asked. "I've never heard that winemaking term before."

"That's because it's not really a winemaking term, just something Carlos Bertonelli used to say. 'Grapes are like children. You want to raise them to be sweet, but not so sweet they overwhelm you.' In other words…"

"A hair shy of precocious."

"Exactly." Tossing a grape into the air, he caught the plump berry in his mouth. "Carlos was full of sayings like that," he said crushing the skin between his teeth. The juice was tart on his tongue; a ways to go before precociousness. "His version of Old World wisdom."

"Signor Bertonelli is the man who used to own these vineyards, right? The ones surrounding the palazzo?"

"*Si.* He was my mentor. Taught me everything I know about winemaking." Nico's heart ached a little every time he thought of the old man, which was often.

"Is that why you're still maintaining the vineyards? Out of respect for him?"

"Out of respect, and partly because Monte Calanetti wouldn't exist without these vineyards. I don't want to see part of our tradition disappear."

There was more to the story, naturally—the truth was always complicated—but Mario didn't need to know how Carlos had kept him grounded when life got crazy. With his even, unflappable demeanor and vat full of wisdom, the old man had been mentor, grandfather and safety net all rolled into one.

When he was a little boy, Nico wondered if the stork hadn't delivered him to the wrong house. That he should have been dropped in the Bertonelli fields instead of his own family's. Truth was, Carlos had been so much more than a mere mentor. Not a day went by that Nico didn't miss the man.

If he were alive, perhaps he could help Nico understand his grandniece better. Looking over the vines to the palazzo, he spied Louisa's platinum-blond hair reflecting the sun as she watched them from the terrace. He nodded hello only to have her move out of view. Still avoiding him. She'd been doing so since the wedding.

Never had he met a woman who was so difficult to read. Cold one moment, warm and tender the next. He'd thought they'd turned a corner at the wedding. A very satisfying corner at that. He smiled, remembering the press of her mouth against his. So soft, so receptive. Then suddenly—poof!—everything changed, and they were back to those frigid early days when she barely gave him the time of day.

"Signor Amatucci?"

Mario was staring at him, obviously waiting for a response of some kind. "Nico," he corrected. "Not *Signor.*"

"Sorry. Nico. I was wondering what you wanted to do next."

Figure out what's going on in my blonde American's head. He doubted that's what Mario meant, though. "I want to gather a few soil samples from the southern fields," he said. "Why don't you head back to the winery and begin testing the grapes we've collected?" It was standard practice to double-check the field readings using the equipment at the lab. Unlike his mentor, Nico liked to have solid data to corroborate his taste buds.

"Are you sure?" Being on the field must truly be making him nostalgic, because the way the kid straightened with the prospect of responsibility brought back memories of the first time Carlos had given him a task to complete on his own. Had he looked that earnest? "I suggested it, didn't I?"

"Yes. Of course. I'll leave the results on your desk."

"Along with your recommendations. I'm eager to hear your suggestions."

The kid nodded again, wide-eyed and serious. "Absolutely."

Of course, Nico would repeat the tests himself later on—the crops were far too valuable to trust to a university student—but there was no need to say anything. Better for Mario's confidence if he believed he was operating without a safety net.

He started packing his test gear back in his canvas satchel. The faded bag had been with him since his days with Carlos, and looked older than that. "If you have any problems, talk to Vitale. I'll be back later this morning."

"How are you getting back? Do you want me to come back for you?"

"No need. I'll hop the wall. There's a low spot," he added when the student frowned. "The Amatuccis and the Bertonellis have been cutting back and forth through these properties for years." At least this Amatucci had. His brother and sister had found other ways to escape.

Once Mario's taillights disappeared in the dust, Nico shouldered his bag and headed south. Above him, the sun lit a cloudless blue sky. The air was ripe with fruit and olives, and if the breeze hit just right, you could catch the faint undertone of lavender. Another perfect day, he thought, wiping the sweat from his forehead.

He was by himself, walking the terraced hill. Back when he was a little boy, these fields had been filled with workers. He remembered the first time he ventured through the archway that divided the properties, a stressed-out, scared boy looking for a place where doors didn't slam and voices were calm. Stepping into the fields of Comparino had been like finding paradise. There was a tranquility in the steady tick-tick-tick of the sprinkler, the low hum of the insects. And it never changed. Oh, there were storms and blights. Natural disasters that caused temporary disruption, but no matter what, Nico knew that come summer, the sounds would be there. Grapes would grow and wine would get made the same as it had for hundreds of years. How he loved the predictability; so unlike the world on his side of the arch, where he never knew from one day to the next whether his parents were together or apart.

Such is the price of grand passion, Carlos said once, after one of his parents' explosive breakups. *It's either sun or storm. No in between.*

Nico wouldn't know. His passion didn't run that deep.

The vines in the south garden had grown thick and tangled with neglect. Left unmolested, insects had nibbled holes in the leaves. Ignoring the bee buzzing near his ear, Nico knelt in the shade. Using his utility knife, he churned the hardened topcoat, unearthing the moist soil beneath. Then he carefully shoveled several inches of the rich black dirt into collection jars. He was wiping the residue on his jeans when a flash of white caught the corner of his eye. He smiled. Part of the reason he'd picked this morning to test the soil was because the southern fields abutted the verandah. This time of morning, Louisa would be having breakfast outside, the way she always did, and while she might be avoiding him, she wouldn't be able to resist spying on what he was doing. Pretending to study the overgrown rose bush marking the end of the row, he kept his back to her. "Careful, *bella mia*," he said, breaking into English, "people might think you are interested in what I am doing."

"I'm always interested in what people do on my property," came the deliciously haughty reply.

Slowly, he turned around. Louisa stood at the railing, a mug cradled between her palms. Despite the early hour, she was fully dressed in jeans and a soft flowing shirt. She hadn't done her hair yet, though. Instead of being pulled tight in her signature severe hairstyle, the strands hung long and loose around her shoulders. If she knew that was how Nico preferred she wear it, she'd no doubt tie it back tighter than ever.

"Do you plan to scrutinize your hotel guests with the same intensity?"

The mention of the hotel was ignored. "I was out here having breakfast. You're the one who crossed into my field of vision."

Apparently they were also going to ignore the fact she'd been watching him earlier. At least she'd answered him. Did that mean they were back on speaking terms?

Only one way to find out. "Breakfast, you say. I don't suppose there is enough coffee for two?" When she didn't immediately answer, he grabbed the terrace balustrades to haul himself up and over the wall.

"I thought you despised American coffee."

"It's growing on me. Like a lot of American things," he added with a smile.

He nodded his head toward the bistro table that held the rest of her meal, including a tall thermal carafe. "Should I drink from the container?"

"Please don't. I'll get you a cup."

She didn't ask him to leave. Did that mean she was thawing again?

"You know that you are going to have to learn how to make a proper espresso if you plan to open a hotel," he said, following her inside.

"I didn't realize you were also an expert on hotel management."

"No, just an expert on being Italian."

As they passed through the glass doors into the room that had been the *piano nobile*, he instinctively paused. "I'll wait here." When Louisa frowned over her shoulder, he lifted his dusty work boot. If Carlos had been alive, he would have walked across the floor without a second thought, but Louisa seemed more the clean and orderly type. The last thing he wanted was to ruin their fragile accord by tracking dirt across the clean terracotta tiles. The gesture must have been appreciated because she nodded rather than arguing the point. "I'll be right back."

The palazzo looked good. Louisa had accomplished a lot over the past few months. The dated furniture had been replaced by comfortable modern pieces but the Old World elegance remained. The intricate coffered ceiling and carved archways gleamed they were so clean. Hard to believe it was the same property. Carlos had never seemed to care about his living conditions, especially after his wife died. And then, of course, there were the years it had sat unclaimed. If Nico hadn't kept an eye on the property, Carlos's legacy would have fallen into even greater shambles.

Louisa never did say why she'd ignored the property for so long. He asked her once, but she told him it was none of his business. And now, after years of neglecting her inheritance, she was breaking her back attempting to return the palazzo to its former glory.

His American was definitely a confusing and complicated woman.

"If you want pastry, you'll have to go home," Louisa said when she returned. "Today is market day."

"Coffee is fine. Thank you." It didn't escape him that she held the cup at arm's length, keeping a healthy distance. Things might be warmer between them, but not completely thawed.

"I'd offer milk, but I know you prefer it black."

"I'm flattered you remember."

"Hard to forget black coffee." She brushed past him, leaving behind a soft memory of Chanel.

"May I ask what you were doing digging in the dirt?"

"Taking soil samples."

"Why?"

For a chance to talk with you. "To determine what needs to be done to make the dirt suitable for new vines." Depending upon the soil levels, he planned to recultivate the field, with canaiolo or cabernet sauvignon, if he was feeling untraditional. "Since it will take a few years before the plants yield a usable harvest, I want to replant sooner rather than later."

"Is that so?" She tossed him a cryptic look before turning to the hills. "Funny. I don't remember selling you the property."

She had to be joking. She was going to claim sovereignty now? "That's funny, because I don't remember you complaining about my maintaining it on your behalf."

"On my behalf and to your benefit. Or are you going to tell me you didn't double your vineyard without paying a penny?"

"No," he replied with a shrug. "Why deny the

truth?" He had benefited from using Carlos's land. Carlos would have wanted as much. "You chose to stay away, and I saw no sense in letting good land go to waste."

"I didn't choose, I…" Whatever she was going to say was swept aside by a deep breath. "Regardless, that doesn't give you the right to do what you want. No matter how good you are at it," she muttered into her cup.

"Good at vineyard management or doing what I want?" Her side eye gave him his answer. "Fine. You're the owner. If you don't want to recultivate, what would you like to do with your neglected vineyards?"

"I'll let you know," she said, jutting her chin for maximum haughtiness.

They both knew he would replant; she was being stubborn for stubbornness' sake. He wondered if she knew how attractive she looked when she was being argumentative. Maybe that was why he enjoyed pushing her buttons. Like a person with a stick poking at a hornet's nest and getting off on the risk, provoking her to annoyance had excitement curling low in his stomach. And damn if it wasn't easy to push her buttons. Seemed as though all he had to do was breathe and her eyes were flashing.

Those eyes were flashing brightly at the moment. Reminding him of how she'd looked right after they kissed.

Ah. Clarity dawned.

"This isn't really about recultivating, is it?" he asked, stepping closer. "This is about what happened at the wedding."

She whipped around to face him. "I told you I didn't want to talk about that."

And yet the moment hung over them begging to be mentioned. "Come now, *bella mia*, don't tell me you expect us to pretend it never happened?"

How could they possibly ignore such an amazing kiss? Surely he wasn't the only one who lay awake at night remembering how perfectly their bodies fit together. The way her breath quickened when he'd stepped closer, told him he wasn't.

"Don't call me *bella mia*, and I'm not asking you to pretend about anything. It's simply not worth talking about. We drank a little too much wine and let the romantic atmosphere get to us, that's all."

"Really?" He leaned in, angling his head near the curve of her neck. "That's all it was? A drunken mistake? I'm not sure I believe you." Especially when her skin flushed from his proximity.

"Why not?"

"Because…" Nico let his gaze take the path his fingers wanted to take. "For one thing, I wasn't drunk."

This time it was Louisa who closed the distance between them, her eyes ablaze from the confrontation. "Maybe you weren't, but that doesn't mean

I wasn't. Much as your ego would like to think otherwise."

Oh, how his little hornet's nest enjoyed poking him as much as he enjoyed poking her. "Trust me, *bella mia*," he said, "my ego doesn't need stroking. Go ahead and call it a drunken mistake if you have to. Same way you can tell yourself that you wouldn't enjoy a repeat performance."

Louisa's lips parted with a gasp, like he knew they would. With a smile curling his own, Nico dipped his head to claim them.

Just as their mouths were about to touch, she turned her face. "Okay, fine, I admit it was a great kiss, but it can't happen again."

"Why not?" Again, he didn't understand. Two people obviously attracted to one another; why shouldn't they explore the possibilities?

"For a lot of reasons. To start with, I'm not looking to get involved in a serious relationship."

All the better. "Neither am I." *Serious* came with certain expectations, and as history had proven, he lacked the depth to meet them.

"And—" she dodged his outstretched hand "—we're neighbors, plus we'll be working on that committee Rafe is creating. We'll be around each other all the time."

"Perhaps I'm misunderstanding, but doesn't that make things easier?"

"It will make things awkward."

"Only as awkward as we let it be," he replied.

Her sandals slapped softly against the floor as she returned to her breakfast table, a position, Nico noted, that put a barrier of glass and wrought iron between them.

Of course, she already knew that, or else her hands wouldn't be gripping the chair back so tightly. Nico knew the cues; she was working up to another reason. "Look, right now I can't be involved with anyone seriously or casually. I need to concentrate on taking care of myself. Do you understand?"

"Si." Better than she realized. The last woman who'd said those words to him had been suffering from a broken heart. Was that Louisa's secret? Had she come to Monte Calanetti because some bastard had let her down?

If that was the case, then far be it for him to add to her injury. One woman was enough to have hurt in a lifetime. There were other women in Monte Calanetti whose company he could keep, even if they weren't as enigmatically fascinating. "Consider the kiss forgotten," he told her.

Louisa's back relaxed as she exhaled. "Thank you," she replied. It felt good to clear the air between them. She'd been acting like a complete brat the past couple of days, stuck between wanting to stand up for herself and being afraid of succumbing to the attraction. She'd treated Nico like the enemy rather than the neighbor she'd come to know and respect. But now that they were on the same page…

Maybe she could finally stop thinking of how much he reminded her of Steven. Her ex-husband's kisses had made her head spin, too, she recalled. The first time she'd been kissed by a man who knew what he was doing.

Feeling Nico's dark eyes studying her, she added in a low voice, "I appreciate your understanding."

"I am nothing if not agreeable."

The joke broke the spell and Louisa laughed. They both knew he could be as stubborn as she could. "Yes, I've seen how agreeable you can be." He'd been particularly "agreeable" earlier this year when his sister, Marianna, had announced her unplanned pregnancy. Louisa had had to talk him out of staking the baby's father in the garden.

"I brought a smile back to your face, did I not?" His smile was crooked and way too sexy.

"I'm glad you said something," he added in a more serious voice. "I did not like that our friendship had turned awkward again."

He was being kind. "I was being a bit irrational, wasn't I?" *Bitchy* would have been a better word.

"A bit. But I may have egged you on."

She laughed. "You think?"

"A bit. How about if we both promise to be on our best behavior?"

"Sounds like a plan."

"Good." To her surprise, there wasn't an ounce of seduction in his smile. If anything he looked genuinely happy. Damn if that didn't make her stomach flutter.

"But," he continued, changing topics, "you should do something about these fields. It is a waste of good cropland."

Not to mention bad business. Guests weren't going to pay to stay at a nonworking vineyard.

Shoot. She was going to have to let him replant, wasn't she? "As soon as I finalize the plans for the hotel, I'll make some decisions." He might be getting his way, but he would get it on her schedule.

"How are your plans going?"

"They're coming along." Only last night she'd put the finishing touches on a preliminary marketing plan.

"Glad to hear it. You know——" he set down his cup, the contents of which, Louisa noticed, were untouched "——my offer still stands. If you need investors…"

Louisa tensed before remembering she'd promised to behave better. It wasn't his fault his offer set her teeth on edge. "I won't need investors," she told him. "I've got a meeting with the bank this afternoon to discuss opening a line of credit. If plans go as I hope, I might be able to open on a limited basis this winter."

"That soon?"

"I did say limited. Waiting until the palazzo is fully renovated could take years, and I want to move fast enough that I can capitalize on the royal wedding." She sounded defensive, the way she used to whenever Steven questioned her. *But he's not Steven, and you don't need anyone's permission anymore.* "I figured I'd concentrate on upgrading the infrastructure, plumbing, electrical, that stuff, and make sure the front half of the palazzo is in perfect working order, before expanding into the back."

"Sounds smart."

"I think so." She did *not* feel a frisson of pleasure at the compliment. "Now I just have to hope the bank comes through with financing quickly." And that the loan officers would take the palazzo for collateral without looking too far beyond the fact she was Carlos Bertonelli's grandniece. Her post-divorce financials were sketchy at best. And heaven help her if the bank looked into her former life. She'd never get financing.

"Who are you meeting with?" Nico asked.

"Dominic Merloni."

"I know him. He's a smart businessman. When I get to my office, I'll call—"

"No. Thank you."

"I don't mind. I'd do the same for any friend."

"Did you do it for Rafe when he opened the restaurant? That's what I thought," she said before he could answer. Rafe would have had his head if he'd interfered.

So would she. "Look, I appreciate your wanting to help, but it's very important to me that I do this 100 percent on my own."

"I understand," he said. Except that he didn't. Louisa could tell from how his brows knit together. He was studying her, looking for the reasons behind her need for independence. Louisa said nothing. She'd already revealed more about her past than he needed to know.

"But," he added, "I hope, if you need a reference, you won't hesitate to give Dominic my name. I'm told I have influence in this town. With some people, that is."

Louisa couldn't help but return his smile. "With some people."

They chatted for a few more minutes, mostly about superficial things. Rafe's committee, plans for the harvest festival. A series of nice safe topics that would prove they'd put the awkwardness of the kiss behind them. Nico had just started describing the traditional grape-stomping ceremony when his cell phone rang.

"Mario, the student who is working for us this summer," he explained when he hung up. "He's finished with the task I assigned him and wondering if I'm coming back before lunch."

"Is it that late?" Louisa looked to her bare wrist.

They'd let time get away from them. Her bank appointment was in the early afternoon.

"Only for people who had breakfast before sunrise," Nico replied. "The rest of the world is safe."

"Good to know, seeing as how I just finished breakfast."

"And my second."

"Such as it was." She nodded to his untouched coffee. "Guess you're not as fond of American coffee as you claimed."

"I must have confused it with something else American, then. Good luck with Dominic." With a parting wink, he jumped over the walk.

He was lucky he didn't break his leg leaping off terraces like that, Louisa thought as she watched him disappear into the vines. She decidedly didn't think about how graceful he looked when he moved. Or about how firm and muscular his arms looked while supporting his weight.

She always did have a weakness for men with nice biceps, she thought with a shiver.

Too bad Nico Amatucci was every mistake she'd vowed not to repeat. She'd had her fill of charismatic, dominating men, thank you very much.

She checked her bare wrist a second time. Her Rolex was long gone—sold to pay off bills—but the habit remained. Didn't matter—Nico's comment about lunch told her the morning was getting on. If she wanted to be prepared for her meeting, she'd best get her act together.

Gathering her plate and the coffee cups, she headed into the palazzo, where the latest draft of her business plan lay spread on the coffee table. Nico must not have noticed, because he wouldn't have been able to resist commenting if he had.

Pausing, Louisa scanned the numbers on the balance sheet with a smile. A solid, thorough plan, but then she'd always been good with numbers. Sadly, she'd forgotten how much she enjoyed working with them. Once upon a time, she'd had a promising career in finance. Until Steven had talked her into staying home shortly after their marriage, that is. Cajoled, really. For appearance's sake, he'd said. People were already gossiping about how the CEO was dating his extremely young employee. Made sense not to add fuel to the fire. "Besides," he'd told her, "as my wife, you have far more important things to focus on."

Like making sure she looked and behaved perfectly at all times. She should have seen the signs then, but she'd been too in love to notice. Lost in her personal fairy tale. The little nobody Cinderella swept off her feet by the silver-haired billionaire Prince Charming.

It wasn't until the feds took him away that she wondered if he hadn't been afraid she'd figure out what he was up to.

Oh well, that was in the past now.

It had taken her a while to settle in at the palazzo, but over the past few months, she'd developed a very comfortable routine. First came breakfast on the terrace, where she would practice her Italian by reading the local papers. The language immersion tape she'd bought in Boston had turned out to be useless—fluent in two weeks, ha!—but nine months in, she was getting pretty comfortable. After breakfast, she would go online to catch up on the American news and check her email. Usually her inbox didn't contain more than a handful of messages, a far cry from the days when she would get note after note. Now her messages were mostly from Dani, who liked to forward jokes and pictures of baby animals. On the plus side, she didn't have to worry about whether the message was some kind of ruse arranged by Steven to catch her in a lie.

At first she didn't look twice at the internet alert, the helpful online tracker she'd created to stay on top of the news. Another reference to the wedding, she assumed. Every day brought two or three mentions. It wasn't until she was about to log off that she realized the alert was one she'd set up before leaving Boston. The words *Louisa Clark* leaped from the screen in boldface type.

Her heart stopped. A year. A whole year without mention. Why now?

She slid her fingers to the mouse. *Please be a coincidence*, she prayed.

And she clicked open the link.

CHAPTER THREE

Scam King's Ex Hosts Royal Wedding
Is Luscious Louisa Looking for a New Partner?

After nine months under the radar, Louisa Clark, the blonde bombshell who seduced and ultimately brought down bogus financier Steven Clark has reappeared. This time in Europe under the name Louisa Harrison...

A BIG FAT PHOTO of her smiling at the royal couple ran under the headline.

The article went on to list her as the owner of Palazzo di Comparino and suggested that hosting the wedding had been her way of snagging a new billionaire husband. Because, after all, that was how she'd landed Steven, right? She was the young femme fatale employee who'd seduced her older boss, only to sell him out when the feds began closing in. Never mind that the narrative didn't remotely resemble the truth. That she was the one who had been seduced and betrayed. Just as long as the story sold papers.

Louisa tried to breathe, but an invisible hand had found its way to her throat and was choking the air out of her. The site even used that god-awful nickname. *Stupid headline writers and their need for memorable alliteration.* No way would this be the only article. Not in the internet era when every gossip blog and newspaper fed off every other.

Sure enough. A few shaky keystrokes later, the search results scrolled down her screen. Some of the stories focused on rehashing the case. Others, though, created all-new speculation. One politician in Florence was even demanding an investigation into the al fresco discovered in the palazzo chapel last summer, claiming it could be part of an elaborate art fraud scheme. Every page turned up more. Headline after headline: Ponzi Scheme Seductress Turns Sights on Tuscany *and* Italy: Lock Up Your Euros! and Royal Scandal! Is Halencia's Financial Future at Stake?

Oh God, Christina and Antonio. She'd turned their fairy-tale wedding into a mockery. They must hate her. Everyone must hate her. Dani. Rafe. *Nico.* They loved Monte Calanetti; all they wanted was for their village to thrive, and she was tainting the town with scandal. How could she ever show her face in town again?

The phone rang. Louisa jumped. *Don't answer*

it. It could be a reporter. Old habits, buried but not forgotten, kicked right in.

Not a reporter, thank goodness. The bank. The name appeared under the number on her call screen. One guess as to why they were calling. Forcing air into her lungs, she answered.

"Signorina Harrison?" an unfamiliar female voice asked.

"Y-yes." Louisa fought to keep her voice from shaking, and lost.

"I'm calling for Signor Merloni. He's asked me to tell you he can't meet with you today. Something has suddenly come up."

"Right. Of course." What a surprise. A lump formed in her throat. Only pride—or maybe it was masochism—made her hang on the line and go through the motions. "Did…did Signor Merloni give you a new date?"

"No, he did not," the woman replied. "I'm afraid his calendar is full for the next several weeks. He's going to have to call you when a time becomes available."

And so the ostracism started. Louisa knew the drill. Signor Merloni wouldn't call back. No one would.

They never did.

Phone dropping from her fingers, Louisa stumbled toward the terrace doors, toward the fresh air and rolling hills she'd come to see as home, only to stop short. Paparazzi could be lurking anywhere, their telephoto lenses poised to snag the next exclusive shot of Luscious Louisa. They could be hiding this moment among the grapevines.

So much for going outside. Backing away, she sank into the cushions when her calves collided with the sofa. What now? She couldn't call anyone. She couldn't go outside.

It was just like before. She was a prisoner in her own home.

Damn you, Steven. Even in prison, he was still controlling her life.

The Brix level matched the portable reading exactly. Nico wasn't surprised. When it came to grapes, he was seldom wrong. *Of course not. Making wine is the only thing you really care about.*

The voice in his head, which sounded suspiciously like his former fiancée's, was wrong. Making wine wasn't the *only* thing he cared about; there was his family, too. And tradition, although tradition involved winemaking so perhaps they were one and the same. Still, while he found great satisfaction in bottling the perfect vintage, if Amatucci Vineyards collapsed tomorrow, he wouldn't collapse in despair. That was his parents' domain. If he couldn't make wine anymore, he would cope, the same way he'd coped when Floriana had walked out on him, or whenever he'd come home to discover his parents had broken up—again. Dispassion, when you thought about it, was a blessing. Heaven knew it had saved him from going mad when growing up.

If the trade-off for sanity meant living a life alone, then so be it.

Why was he even thinking about this? Louisa's comment about needing time for herself, that's why. Someone had hurt Louisa badly enough that she'd fled to Italy. Her pain was too close to the mistakes he'd made with Floriana. Poor, sweet Floriana. He'd tried so hard to want her properly, but his tepid heart wouldn't—couldn't.

Was the man who'd broken Louisa's heart trying to be something he wasn't, too? Hard to believe a man would throw her over for any other reason.

"Mario, could you turn down the volume?" he hollered. He could hear the television from in here.

Leaving the beakers he'd been measuring on his lab table, he left his office and walked into the main processing area where Mario and his production manager, Vitale, stood watching the portable television they had dragged from the break room.

"Last time I checked, football didn't need to be played at top volume," he said. With the equipment being readied for harvest, it didn't take much for the noise to reverberate through the empty plant. He motioned for Giuseppe to hand him the remote control. "I didn't know there was a match today."

"Not football, *signor*, the news," Mario replied.

"You brought the television in here to watch the *news*?" That would be a first. Football reigned supreme.

"Si," Giuseppe replied. "Vitale's wife called to say they were talking about Monte Calanetti."

Again? Nico would have thought they were done discussing the royal wedding by now. "Must be a slow news…" He stopped as Louisa's face suddenly appeared on the screen. It wasn't a recent photo, she was far more dressed up than usual, and it showed her with a man Nico didn't recognize. A very handsome man, he noticed, irritably.

The caption beneath read Luscious Louisa— Back Again?

Luscious Louisa?

"Isn't that the woman who owns the palazzo?" Vitale looked over at him.

Nico didn't answer, but the news reader droned on. "…key witness in prosecuting her husband, Steven Clark, for investment fraud and money laundering. Clark is currently serving seventy-five years…"

He remembered reading about the case. Clark's pyramid scheme had been a huge scandal. Several European businessmen had lost millions investing with him. And Louisa had been his wife and testified against him?

No wonder she'd run to Italy.

Another picture was on the screen; one from the royal wedding. Nico gritted his teeth as a thousand different emotions ran through him. The presenter was talking about Louisa as if she were some kind of siren who'd led Clark to his doom. Had they met the woman? Alluring, yes, but dishonest? Corrupt?

His ringtone cut into his thoughts. Keeping his eyes on the television, he pulled his phone from his back pocket.

"Have you seen the news?" Dani asked when he answered.

"Watching it right now," he replied. On-screen, the presenter had moved on to a different headline.

"The story's on every channel. It's all anyone in the restaurant can talk about."

It's untrue, he corrected silently. The ferocity of his certainty surprised him. He had not one shred of evidence to support his belief, and yet he knew in his bones that Louisa wasn't guilty of anything. One merely had to look in her eyes to know that whatever the press said, they didn't have the entire story.

"Did you know?" he asked Dani. Rafe's wife was Louisa's closest friend. If Louisa had told anyone of her past...

"No. She never talks about her life before she got here," Dani answered. "Hell, she barely talks about herself."

Nico's gut unclenched. Silly, but he'd felt strangely hurt at the idea of Louisa sharing her secrets with someone else.

"There are reporters all over town," Dani continued. "One even came in here asking questions. I've been trying to call her since the story broke to see if she's okay, but she's not answering her phone."

"Probably avoiding the press."

"I'm worried, though. She's so private, and to have her life story plastered all over the place…"

Terrifying. "Say no more," he replied. "I'll head right over."

Louisa had lost track of the time. Curled in the corner of her sofa, away from the windows, she hugged her knees and tried to make her brain focus on figuring out the next step. Obviously, she couldn't stay in Monte Calanetti. Not without tainting the village with her notoriety. And going back to Boston…well, that was out of the question. What would she do? Go to her mother's house and listen to "I told you so" all day long?

Louisa hugged herself tighter. Ever since seeing the media alert, there'd been a huge weight on her chest, and no matter how hard she tried to take a deep breath, she couldn't get enough air. It was as though the walls were closing in, the room getting smaller and smaller. She didn't want to leave. She liked her life here. The palazzo, the village…they were just starting to feel like home.

She should have known it wouldn't last. Steven's shadow was destined to follow her everywhere. For the rest of her life, she would be punished for falling in love with the wrong man.

"...you're doing?" A giant crash followed the question. The sound of tinkling glass forced Louisa to her feet. Running to the terrace door, she peered around the corner of the door frame in time to see Nico dragging a stranger across the terrace toward the wall. The crash she'd heard was her breakfast table, which now lay on its side, the top shattered.

"Hey, what do you think you're doing?" she heard the stranger gasp. "This is my exclusive."

"Exclusive this," Nico growled. Holding the man's collar in one hand, he yanked the expensive camera the man carried from around his neck and hurled it over the wall.

"Bastard! You're going to pay for that."

"Be glad it was only your camera." Nico yanked the man to his feet only to shove him against the railing. "Now get out. And if I ever see your face in the village again, you'll find out exactly what else I'm capable of breaking, understand?" He shoved the man a second time, with a force that made Louisa, still hidden behind the door frame, jump. Whatever the reporter said must have satisfied him, and Nico released his grip on the man's shirt. Louisa stepped back as the man started toward the stairs.

"Where are you going?" Nico asked, his hand slapping down on the man's shoulder. "Leave the way you came in."

"Are you kidding? That's a five-foot drop."

"Then I suggest you brace yourself when you land." The two men stared at one another for several seconds. When it became obvious Nico wasn't backing down, the reporter hooked a leg over the railing.

"I'm calling my lawyer. You're going to pay for that camera."

"Call whoever you'd like. I'll be glad to explain how I'm calling the police to report you for trespassing on private property. Now are you leaving, or shall I throw you over that railing?"

The reporter did what he was told, disappearing over the rail. Slowly Louisa stepped into the light. Nico's shoulders were rising and falling in agitated breaths, making her almost afraid to speak. "Is he gone?" she asked in a soft voice.

"Is he the first one?" he asked, voice rough.

He turned, and the dark fury Louisa saw on his face had her swallowing hard to keep the nerves from taking over her throat. She nodded. "I think so."

"He was climbing over the wall when I got here. Probably saw your terrace door was open and thought he could catch you up close and off guard."

"In Boston, they preferred using telephoto lenses."

"You're not in Boston anymore."

"I know." She should have realized how ruthless

the press would be. After all, this was Italy; they'd invented the word *paparazzi*.

"At least you won't have to worry about this one trespassing again. That is, if he's smart."

"Thanks."

"Can't promise there won't be more, though," he said brushing past her. "You'd best be prepared."

More. He was right, there would be others. It was all she could do not to collapse in a heap where she stood. Those months of hiding in Boston had nearly destroyed her. She wasn't up to another go-round. The stranger on her terrace was proof enough of that. If Nico hadn't shown up when he did…

Why had he shown up? Returning to her living room, where she found her neighbor searching through the bookshelf cabinets. "What are you doing?"

"Carlos kept a stash of fernet tucked in back of one of these cabinets. Do you still have it?"

"Two doors to the left." She hadn't gotten around to finding a better location. "I meant why are you here?"

"Dani called me. She saw the news on television."

"Let me guess, she's horrified to find out who she's been friends with and wants me to stay away so I won't drag the restaurant into it." Seeing the same darkness on Nico's face that she'd seen a few moments ago, it would seem her neighbor felt the same way.

"What? No. She and Rafe are trying to figure out what's going on. A reporter came to the restaurant asking questions." He paused while he pulled a dust-covered bottle from the cabinet. "She said she tried calling you a half dozen times."

That explained some of the phone calls then. "I wasn't answering the phone."

"Obviously. They asked if I would come over and make sure you were okay. Good thing, too, considering you were about to have an unwanted visitor."

He filled his glass and drank the contents in one swallow. "This is the point in our conversation where you suggest that I'm an unwanted visitor."

"What can I say? I'm off my game today." She sank into her corner and watched as Nico drank a second glass. When he finished, he sat the empty glass on a shelf and turned around. He wore a much calmer expression now. Back in control once again.

"Why didn't you say anything about your former husband?" he asked.

And say what? *My ex is Steven Clark. You know, the guy who ran the billion-dollar investment scam. I'm the wife who turned him in. Maybe you've read about me? They call me Luscious Louisa?* She plucked at the piping on one of the throw pillows. "The idea was to make a fresh start where no one knew anything about me," she replied."

"You know how unrealistic that is in this day and age?"

"I managed it for nine months, didn't I?" She offered up what she hoped passed for a smile. Nine wonderful months. Almost to the point where she'd stopped looking over her shoulder.

When he didn't smile back, she changed the subject. "You said a reporter came into the restaurant?"

"This morning. That's how Dani knew to turn on the television."

She could just imagine the questions he'd asked, too. "Tell them I'm sorry. Things will die down once they realize I'm not in Monte Calanetti anymore."

Nico's features darkened again. "What are you talking about?"

"I'm catching the bus to Florence tonight."

"You're running away?"

He made it sound like a bad thing. "I certainly can't stay. Not anymore."

"But the palazzo... What about all your plans for restoring the property and turning it into a hotel? Surely, you're not planning to abandon Palazzo di Comparino *again*?"

His voice grew harsh on the last word, causing Louisa to cringe. His feelings regarding the palazzo were no secret; to him, the fact she allowed the property to sit unclaimed for so long was as big a crime as anything Steven had done. Of course, she had good reason for the delay, but he didn't know that.

"Have you seen what they are writing about me?"

she asked him. The stories would only get worse. "That guy you threw off my terrace is probably down in the village right now trying to dig up dirt. And what he can't find, he'll make up. Whatever he can do to sell papers."

"So?"

"So, I'm doing Monte Calanetti a favor by leaving. The town is on an economic high. I don't want to do anything to take that away." Unable to stand the way his eyes were bearing down on her, Louisa pushed herself to her feet and walked toward the rear corner of the room, as far from the windows— and Nico—as possible. A tapestry hung on the wall there, and she focused on the intricate weave of brown thread. "Better I leave the palazzo empty than stay and let the town become branded as the home of Luscious Louisa," she said.

"How noble of you, running away without saying goodbye to your friends. I mean, that's what you were going to do, no? Leave without saying goodbye?"

"Like people would care." Rejection hurt enough when it was people you didn't like. The idea of walking down the street and seeing disdain in the eyes of people she cared about made her sick to her stomach. "Trust me, everyone will be more than happy to see me gone."

"Happy? Did you say we would be happy?" There was the sound of footsteps, and suddenly a hand was on her shoulder, yanking her around and bringing her face-to-face with a pair of flashing brown eyes. So angry; so ready to correct her.

It was instinctive. The corner of her vision caught his hand starting to rise, and she couldn't help it.

She flinched.

Madonna mia, did she think he was going to strike her? As he raked his fingers through his hair—completing the motion he'd started before Louisa recoiled—Nico felt his hand shaking. What scared him was that he did want to hit something. Not Louisa. Never Louisa. But something. The wall. That miserable paparazzo's face. So much for the liquor calming his nerves. The swell of anger that he'd been fighting since seeing the news was pushing hard against his self-control. Mixing with another emotion, one he couldn't identify but that squeezed his chest like a steel band, the feelings threatened to turn him into someone he didn't recognize.

How could she just leave Monte Calanetti? For nine months they'd treated her as one of their own, made her part of their family, and she didn't think they cared? Did she truly think so little of them?

He felt betrayed. "If you think so little of us that you believe we would let a few gossip articles sway our opinion, then perhaps you should go somewhere else," he said. "After all these months, you should now have realized that people in Monte Calanetti are smarter than that."

"That include Dominic Merloni?"

The banker? What did he have to do with anything?

"He canceled our meeting as soon as the news broke. He won't be the only person to cut me off. Just the first."

"Dominic Merloni is an arrogant bastard who thinks everyone in the village should worship him because he once played football for Genoa."

"That's not what you said about him this morning."

"This morning I was being polite." But if she was going to be irrational, then there was no need to keep up the pretense. "I'm talking about the people who matter. Like Dani, your supposed *best friend*. You think she is so petty?"

"Of course not," she replied. "But Dani loves everybody."

"Yes, she does, but you were going to leave her without saying goodbye anyway."

"I already told you, I'm—"

"Yes, yes, doing the village a favor. Let us start organizing the benediction. Saint Louisa the martyr. Abandoning Palazzo di Comparino for the good of the people."

Louisa stood with her arms wrapped around her as though they were the only thing holding her up.

As far from the woman he'd come to know as could be. Where was the haughty American who challenged him on every turn? The hornet who threatened every time he poked her nest? "I don't know why you care so much," she muttered.

Nico didn't know either, beyond the emotions that continued squeezing his chest. He shouldn't care at all. He should accept the change in circumstance as another one of life's upheavals and move on.

He couldn't, though. All he could think about was how the more he watched her retreat into herself, the more he wanted to grab her by the shoulders and shake the fight back into her. He wanted to…to…

He stalked back to the bookshelf. Grabbing a clean glass from the bar, he poured two more glasses of fernet and walked back to her. "Here," he said, holding one of the glasses out. "Drink. Maybe you'll start thinking more clearly." Maybe he would, too.

"I don't need to think clearly," she replied. Nonetheless, she took the drink. "I need to leave town."

"And go where?"

"I don't know. Africa. New Zealand. Someplace where they can't find me. I'll figure something out. I just know I have to leave.

"No, damn it!" he said, slamming the bottle on the shelf. "You can't!"

The air between them crackled with tension. Nico looked at Louisa cradling her glass with trembling hands and grew ashamed. Since when did he yell and slam objects?

Taking a deep breath, he began again, this time making sure his voice remained low and level. "Leaving town is the worst thing you can do."

"How can you say that?"

Again, Nico wasn't entirely sure. Several answers came to mind, but none of them felt completely whole or honest. The true, complete answer remained stuck in the shadows, unformed.

"Because the town needs you," he said, grabbing the first reason that made sense. "You've become an important part of our community. Whether you believe in them or not—" she turned away at his pointed dig "—the people here believe in you."

"Besides," he added in a voice that was even lower than before, "if you run away, the press win. People will believe what's written—the stories will start to sound true. Is that what you want? To give Luscious Louisa life?"

"No."

"Then stay, and show the world you've got nothing to hide. That what the press is saying is nothing more than gossip."

He let his reasoning wash over her. For several minutes, she said nothing, all her concentration focused on an invisible spot inside her drink. When she finally spoke, the words were barely a whisper. "What if you're wrong?"

"I'm not." It hurt to hear the doubt in her voice. Damn her ex for killing her trust. "Whatever happens, you already have three people on your side."

"But last time..." She shook her head.

"Last time there was a trial, no? This time it is only gossip. In a few days the press will have moved on to a new scandal and forgotten all about Luscious Louisa. Then you go back to your life. Surely, you can handle a few days of whispers, can't you?"

"You have no idea how many whispers I've handled in my lifetime," she replied, looking up at last.

Finally, there was a spark. A bit of the fire he'd come to expect. "Good. Then, it's settled. You're staying here, where you belong."

Louisa had opened her mouth to reply but stopped abruptly. He heard the sound of rustling outside on the terrace. She'd heard it, too, because the fingers holding her glass grew white with tension.

For the third time in less than an hour Nico could feel his temper rise. At this rate he would need an entire case of fernet to keep him from murdering the entire Italian media corps.

"Wait here," he mouthed, then held an index finger to his lips. Moving as softly as possible, he headed toward the terrace door, which they'd accidentally left propped open, and peered around the corner. There was another rustle, followed by a flutter before a lark flew past his face. Nico started at the sudden movement, his cheeks turning hot. "Just a bird," he said unnecessarily.

"This time," Louisa replied.

She was right. This time. Sooner or later the paparazzi would get their shot. "Maybe you should stay with Dani and Rafe," he said.

"I thought you didn't want me running away."

"I don't, but I also want you safe." He didn't say it, but it wasn't only the paparazzi he was worried about. There were also those unhinged few who would want to see if Luscious Linda was as sexy as the gossip pages implied. Until the story died down, trespassers were a real threat.

"I don't know…"

Surely they were past her insecurity at this point, weren't they? "What's the problem? As long as you are staying with them, you won't have to worry about the paparazzi. Rafe will make sure no one bothers you." Nico would make sure he did.

"Rafe and Dani have a business to run. I'm not going to ask them to waste their time babysitting me."

"No one is babysitting anyone."

"Aren't they? If they have to spend their time protecting me from all the paparazzi in town then it's babysitting," Louisa replied. "I'm better off grabbing the bus." She took a sip of her drink and grimaced. "What is this stuff?"

"Fernet-Branca."

"I hate peppermint," she replied, and set the glass on the coffee table.

"It is an acquired taste." Her change of topic wasn't going to work. She could complain about the drink all she wanted, he wasn't going to let her leave Monte Calanetti.

Tossing back his own drink, he slapped the glass down before the liquor even started cooling his insides. "If you don't want to stay with Rafe and Dani," he said, "then you'll just have to stay with me."

"Excuse me?"

If the situation weren't so serious, he'd laugh at the shock on her face. It was the perfect solution, though. "You will be able to avoid the paparazzi in the village, plus you'll be close enough to keep an eye on the palazzo. Can you think of a better location?"

"Hell. When it freezes over."

This time he did laugh. Here was the feisty Louisa he was used to.

"I'm serious," she said. "If I don't want Rafe and Dani playing babysitter, I sure as hell don't want you doing it.

She was being stubborn again. It wouldn't work any more than trying to change the subject had. "Fine. If it makes you feel better, you can work while you are staying with me."

"Work?"

"Yes. I told you, since the wedding, we've been

inundated with orders for Amatucci Red. I can barely keep up as it is, and with the harvest and the festival coming up, I'm going to need as much help as I can get. Unless you don't think you can handle filing invoices and processing orders."

"You—you'd trust me to do that?"

"Why wouldn't I?"

"What about Luscious Louisa?"

God, how it hurt to see her looking so vulnerable. Tears rimming her eyes and her lower lip trembling. Silently, he damned Steven Clark for dragging her down with him.

He might have promised to keep his distance, but at this moment, he couldn't stop himself from closing the space between them. He brushed his thumb across her quivering lip.

"Like I told you before, anyone who has spent time with you knows you're not the icy seductress the press makes you out to be."

"Thank you." A tear slipped out the corner of her eye and he fanned it away with his hand. So vulnerable and so beautiful. It shocked him how badly he suddenly needed to keep her safe. But then, this afternoon had been full of shocking reactions he'd never experienced before.

There was one reaction he recognized, though. The stirring in his jeans as he breathed in her scent. He brushed the hair from her face, the strands reminding him of corn silk. Promise be damned. He wanted to kiss her. Quickly, he stepped away before he could take action. Now was not the time to push his luck. "Go pack a bag," he told her. "We'll leave before the paparazzi realize you're gone."

You made the right decision, Louisa reminded herself on the way upstairs. Hiding out *was* better than running away, and Amatucci Vineyards did make the ideal hiding place. Plus she would be earning her keep. It wasn't as though she was going to become Nico's kept woman. She'd insist on the entire arrangement being professional and platonic.

Why, then, was her stomach in knots? Maybe, she thought as her eyes fell on the suitcase in the corner, because she'd gone from leaving town to working for Nico in less than an hour without knowing how she made the journey.

Or maybe it was because saying yes had become a whole lot easier once Nico had brushed her cheek.

CHAPTER FOUR

Luscious Louisa's Latest Conquest?

"Too bad they couldn't find a proper synonym. *Conquest* spoils the alliteration." Nico said, turning the newspaper over.

Louisa didn't share his sense of humor. The headline screamed across the front page along with a photograph of her and Nico cropped from one of the official wedding shots. Apparently the photographer Nico kicked off her balcony had done some research following the altercation. The article described how the "enraged" vintner had come to her rescue and implied the two of them had been an item for weeks. Or, as the article put it, she'd managed to charm the richest man in town.

This was exactly what she didn't need after a restless night. There was still a large part of her dying to grab the first bus to Florence. Screaming loudly, in fact. She couldn't stop thinking how easily she had agreed to Nico's idea. Sure, he had a point about staying and proving the press wrong, but to put herself in his care like this? It reminded her of how things had begun with Steven. He'd liked to swoop in and take care of everything when they were dating, too. *Only you're not dating Nico*, she reminded herself, staring down at her breakfast pastry.

And unlike with Steven, this time she had age and hindsight in her favor. She may have agreed to stay here, but she would keep her bags packed. That way if the situation changed and the walls started closing in, she could be out of here in a flash.

Meanwhile, her breakfast partner was enjoying his pastry as though he didn't have a care in the world.

"I don't know how you can be so cavalier," she said watching him chew his pastry. Anyone would think he liked being dragged through the tabloid mud.

Nico shrugged. "How am I supposed to act?"

Indignant, perhaps? Angry? Some *show* of emotion. He'd practically exploded when he discovered the paparazzo yesterday, and that had nothing to do with him. These headlines were personal. "The article makes you sound like a lovesick fool."

"Which anyone who knows me will immediately recognize as a complete fabrication. I'm not and have never been the lovesick type."

A fact that should comfort her, seeing as how she

was now sleeping under his roof. It didn't, though. Instead, she felt a dull ache in the pit of her stomach.

"So what was yesterday? An anomaly?"

He looked away. "Yesterday I caught a man breaking into your home. I was upset for your safety. This," he said as he waved his cup over the tabloid "is entirely different."

"How? It's still an invasion of privacy. And the things they wrote about us…" As though Nico were some kind of fly trapped in her web. She shivered. "Surely you care what people think."

"I already told you, anyone who knows me will recognize it for the garbage it is."

"Why is that?" Not that she wasn't glad, but she wanted to know why he was so certain.

A strange shadow appeared behind his eyes, turning them darker than usual. "Like I said, I'm not the lovesick kind," he replied. "Now, the fact they referred to me as the 'royal vintner'? That is something I hope people *will* believe. You cannot buy better publicity."

"Glad you're happy." One of them should be.

She took a look around the surroundings that were to be her home away from home for the next few days. Worn out and uncomfortable last night, she'd insisted on being shown straight to her room. Nico's rust-and-green kitchen was warm but dated, like the kitchen of a man who didn't spend too many meals at home. Did that mean he didn't entertain much either? Would people notice he had company?

A sudden, horrifying thought struck her. Now that Nico had been identified, the press would start stalking him, too. For all they knew, a telephoto lens could be trained on them right now. Reflexively, she looked over her shoulder at the kitchen window.

"Relax," Nico told her. "I drew the curtains when we got home last night. No one can see you."

Sure, they couldn't see her now. But eventually… "This was a mistake. I'm better off just going to Florence."

"No one is going anywhere except to the winery." Nico's hand reached across the table and grabbed her wrist, preventing her from standing. "Trust me, everything is going to be fine. In a few days, another scandal will erupt and the press will forget all about you."

Louisa looked down at the bronzed hand gently encircling her arm. His thumb brushing her pulse point, the tiny movement as soothing as a caress. That his slightest touch could calm her was disturbing in itself.

Slipping free, Louisa reached for the newspaper and flipped it back over. The picture on the front page showed the two of them with their heads together in quiet conversation. Arm slung casually over the back of her chair, he was leaning forward as she spoke in his ear, her hand resting lightly on his forearm. She remembered the moment. The orchestra had started playing, and she'd moved closer so she could comment on the song selection. Thanks to the angle, they looked more like a couple who had eyes only for each other.

A second photo greeted her when she turned the page. The two of them dancing. No need to mess with the angle this time. Their gazes were locked; their bodies pressed together like lovers'. Must have been taken only moments before Nico had kissed her.

What if there was a photo of them kissing? Louisa's stomach dropped. The blogosphere would have a field day. Her horror must have shown on her face, because when she looked up, Nico was watching her. "If they had a photo, they would have used it," he said, reading her mind.

He was right, Louisa thought, letting out her breath. "The one they used is bad enough. Did we really look like that?" Like they couldn't get close enough.

"Considering what followed, I would have to say yes."

That's what she was afraid of. Louisa dropped her head on her arms with a groan. "It's only a couple of photographs," he said, patting the back of her head. "We'll survive."

He didn't understand. Any photograph was one photograph too many. "Believe it or not," she said, lifting her head, "there was a time when I liked having my picture taken." She remembered her first public date with Steven and how the local press surrounded them. She'd felt like someone had dropped her on a Hollywood red carpet. "I thought being featured in the paper was the coolest thing ever."

Letting out a long breath, she balanced her chin on the back of her hand. "After Steven was arrested, reporters started camping out in cars across the street. They'd call my name each time I left the house, and I would hear the cameras snapping. Click-click-click-click. It never stopped. After a while I stopped going out unless it was to go to court. I had my food delivered. I kept the curtains drawn. I swear Steven had more freedom in prison." Out of the corner of her eye, she caught Nico's gaze slide toward his windows and the green linen drapes blocking the view.

"Did you know, I couldn't even take out my garbage, because they would go through the contents?" she asked. "I had to let it pile up in the basement until after the trial was over." If she concentrated, she could smell the stench. The horrible sour smell that drifted up the stairs every time she opened the basement door. "I actually dreamt once that the bags overflowed and buried me alive."

"Bella mia…" He reached for her hand.

Louisa pulled back with a shake of her head. No more comforting touches. "I wasn't trying to make you feel sorry for me." Honestly, she didn't know why she'd told him at all. The memory had simply popped out and it had been the first time she shared the secret with anyone. She supposed it was because the situation was repeating itself again now.

"Well, I promise no garbage here."

How was it he knew the way to make her smile no matter how aggravated or sad she got? "Well, if there is," she said, "you're responsible for taking it out."

"Agreed." Nico smiled, and the warmth in his eyes was as reassuring as any embrace. For that moment, anyway, Louisa felt as if everything would be okay.

Seeing Louisa smile cheered him. It was strange how important seeing her smile was becoming to him. Nico tried to imagine what it must have been like for her during the trial, trapped inside her home while the wolves with their cameras gathered around in wait.

It made him doubly glad that he had lied about the photographs not bothering him. He would never tell Louisa, but seeing the pictures actually bothered him a great deal, although not for the reason she thought. It was his expression in the photographs, a dazed, trancelike appearance that upset him the most. He'd been photographed by the press dozens of times, but never could he remember seeing a shot where he could be seen looking so intently at his partner. Then again, he couldn't remember ever sharing a dance as memorable as the one he shared with Louisa either. Looking at the photograph had brought every detail back into focus, from the softness of her silk gown to the floral scent of her hairspray as she curled into his neck.

Unfortunately, Louisa's reaction was far different. Even though he expected her to get upset, he was surprised at the disappointment her response left in his stomach. Clearly, being the one who usually kept the emotional distance, Nico wasn't used to a woman's disinterest.

Sensing her attention about to return to the headlines, Nico gathered the newspaper and folded it in two. "No more gossip," he said, slapping the paper on the countertop. "We move on to better topics. You need to finish your breakfast. Today is a workday. If you're serious about earning your keep, then we need to get to the winery."

"Are you always this bossy with your houseguests?" she asked, the smile staying in place.

"Only the Americans," Nico countered. What would she say if she discovered she was the first woman to be one of his houseguests? Not even Floriana had been given such an honor. Since his parents had moved away, Nico had preferred the house to remain a place of peace and tranquility, something it had never been when he was a child.

And didn't Louisa, with her damp hair and bare feet, look as if she belonged to the place. The novelty of having company, he decided. Other women would look equally at home, if he ever bothered to invite them.

But would other women engender such a strong desire to protect them? Last night, he'd literally found himself patrolling the house, and again first thing this morning. Frankly, he was surprised he hadn't stood guard outside Louisa's bedroom door to keep her safe.

Keep her safe or keep her from leaving? The dread that gripped him when she mentioned going to Florence was no less today than it had been yesterday. He wished he understood why her leaving Monte Calanetti disturbed him so much.

He looked past her shoulder to the back door and the thin dark line scored in the wood just to the left of the doorknob. A reminder of the time his mother had thrown a carving knife at his father's disappearing back. "Did you sleep well?" he heard himself ask.

"Okay," she said. "It's never easy sleeping the first night in a new place and all."

"Perhaps, after a full day's work, tonight will be better." For both of them. Wiping his mouth, he tossed the napkin onto his empty plate and stood up. "Speaking of…we have a busy day. Get your shoes on and I'll show you what you'll be doing for me."

* * *

Beyond the vineyards themselves, Amatucci Vineyards had two primary sections. There was a medieval stone villa that housed the store and wine-tasting rooms as well as a modern production facility. It was to the second building that Nico and Louisa headed, cutting through the rear garden and vines. Something else Louisa had been too stressed out to appreciate yesterday. Unlike the villa, which was stately and ripe with family heirlooms, Nico's garden was a breathtaking display of natural beauty. The vines draping the pergola beams had minds of their own, their branches dipping and weaving into a unique overhead tapestry. Likewise, urns had been placed around the terracotta terrace, their roses and olive plants spiraling up cedar trellises with stunning wildness.

"I like to be reminded of how rugged the hills can be," Nico said when she complimented him. *Rugged* was a good word and fit him perfectly, she thought, dodging a low-hanging branch. Nico was earthy and independent. Civilized, but not completely.

"Most of the employees are in the field at this time of day," Nico told her as he unlocked the facility door. "I'll set you up in one of the back offices so you'll have maximum privacy. I also sent an email to the staff last night reminding them that I expect professionalism and discretion at all times, and that I won't tolerate gossip."

"Sounds like you've thought of everything." *Swooping in to take control...* A tightness found its way into her stomach, which she immediately pushed aside. *Not the same thing*, she silently snapped. *Stop comparing.*

The door opened into a small receiving room dominated by filing cabinets and a cluttered metal desk at which a lanky young man too big for his chair sat reading. Behind him a glass window looked out over a warehouse-sized room full of gleaming stainless-steel processing machines.

He practically jumped to his feet when he heard Nico shut the door. "*Signor!* I was just—just—" Seeing Louisa, he stopped midsentence and simply stared. This morning's newspaper lay open on the desk, the photo of her and Nico on display.

"Good morning, Mario. I'd like you to meet Louisa Harrison from Palazzo di Comparino. She's offered to help us fulfill shipping orders so we can get ready for harvest."

"Hello."

"Mario is studying viticulture at the university. He wants to learn how to become a great vintner."

Mario was doing his best to look anywhere but at her. Still, if Nico could breeze in here and act as though there wasn't a suggestive photo of them lying a foot away, then so could she. Mustering up some fake confidence, she flashed the young man a smile. "Pleasure to meet you, Mario," she said holding out her hand.

"Um, yes. Likewise," Mario muttered. Still avoiding her gaze, he hurriedly shook her hand before picking up a stack of paperwork. "I'd better finish getting these field readings recorded into the system," he said. Clasping the papers to his chest, he rushed out of the office.

"Told you people would have problems with me," she said once the young man disappeared.

Nico's mouth was a thin tight line. "I will talk to him. Let him know that kind of behavior is unacceptable."

"Don't. It's not his fault."

"But of course it is. I won't have my employees treating you poorly. He needs to know that."

"Please." She grabbed his hand as he headed toward the door. "I don't want to make a scene." Mario's behavior was nothing compared to what she'd endured in Boston. What she didn't want was to feel as though she was under an even bigger spotlight. "Just show me where I'm supposed to sit and let me get to work."

"You're going to stay, then? I don't have to talk you out of leaving?"

"For now." She was here. She might as well try to tough it out for a little while. After all, there was always the chance Mario was just shy or something, right?

The way Nico's face brightened helped, too, as did his softly spoken "I'm glad."

"But, before I bring you to your office," he added, "I want to show you the facility. You should know your way around the building if I'm not here and you need to find something."

The office exited into the main plant. Standing on the landing just outside the office door, Louisa was shocked to see the facilities empty.

"Where is everybody?" she asked.

"I always close right before harvest. Gives the employees time with their families and lets me make sure the equipment is in working order. Enjoy the silence while you can. Come next week this building will be so loud you won't be able to hear yourself think."

"I bet." She didn't have a clue what any of the machines did, but simply given the sheer number of machines she'd expect a lot of noise. "It all looks so modern," she remarked. "Not quite how I expected wine to be made."

"No doubt you pictured a dark cavern full of oak casks where a group of Italian gypsy women crush the grapes by foot?"

"Nothing that dramatic."

"Are you sure? That's what the tourists believe. Why do you think my store is in the oldest building on the property? To continue the myth."

Meanwhile, their Old World wine was being produced in the finest of twenty-first-century stainless-steel and concrete surroundings. "So no grape stomping at all, then?" Louisa asked as she followed him down the stairs and onto the plant floor.

"Only at the harvest festival."

Ahead, they caught the flash of a pale blue work shirt near one of the machines. "Vitale," Nico called out. "Is that you?"

A silver head appeared. "Yes, *signor*. I was replacing the timer belt." Just like Mario had, the man avoided looking in her direction. "You were right, *signor*," he said. "It had worn thin. We shouldn't have any more problems."

"Good. Good. Vitale, I'd like you to meet Louisa." Once again, Nico forced an introduction, and again Louisa was acknowledged with a nervous smile and a nod before Nico offered Vitale an excuse to leave.

"Give them time," Nico told her when she started to comment. "They'll warm up to you."

Sure they will, she thought with a sigh. "People are going to believe what they want to believe, Nico." Sometimes even when the truth was right in front of them—the way she had with Steven. "And in this case, the headlines have had way too big a head start."

"Headlines be damned. Once they get to know you, they'll realize what is written in the papers is garbage. In a few weeks no one in Monte Calanetti will even care about Luscious Louisa."

"From your lips…"

While they were talking, he'd moved closer, narrowing the space between them until he stood no more than a foot away. Close enough she could see the dark hair peering out from the open collar of his shirt and smell the spicy citrus of his aftershave. "Louisa," he said, his gentle voice sounding as though he were stating the simplest of truths. "It doesn't take a rocket scientist to see the truth about a person."

"Don't be so sure. There's an entire town back in Massachusetts that could prove you wrong."

Nico chuckled. Despite the gap between them, his fingers had somehow found their way into her hair and were combing the strands away from her face. "You're being dramatic, *bella mia*. I'm sure your true friends knew better."

"They might have, if I'd had any."

"What are you talking about?"

"Nothing." Distracted by his touch, she'd opened a door she hadn't meant to open. "Like you said, I'm being dramatic."

He didn't believe her, but Louisa didn't care. She'd revealed enough secrets for one day.

"I'm tired," she said instead. "It's making me say silly things."

"You should get some rest, then."

Easier said than done. True *rest* had eluded her for years. The last time she'd relaxed—truly relaxed—had been when? The first few months of her marriage? Such a long time ago.

Dear Lord, but she was tired of being on guard, and Nico's touch felt so wonderfully comforting. With a soothing brush of his hand, her resistance slipped a little further. It felt so good having someone on her side. Nico's shoulder was right there. Broad, capable, strong. Would it be so bad if she leaned on him for just a little bit? She was so very tired of being alone.

With a soft sigh escaping her lips, she curled into him.

"It's all right," she heard Nico whisper as his arms wrapped around her. "I'm here. I'll take care of everything."

This was a first for Nico. Taking a woman in his arms without any intention of making love to her. But as he drew her close, her sweet floral scent wrapping itself around him, his only thought was of reassurance. He knew why, of course. Louisa's cool and distant mask had slipped, and the vulnerability he saw deepened the queer sense of protectiveness she'd awakened in him. Every time, the depth of what he was feeling shocked him. What was it about this blonde American that made him want to fly to America and strangle every reporter in the country personally for causing her such pain?

At least he could make sure the European press didn't copy their American colleagues, even if he had to physically throw every paparazzo in Italy off his property. Cradling her head against his shoulder, he whispered. "It's all right. I'll take care of everything."

Instantly, she stiffened. "No," she said pulling out of his embrace. "Don't."

Nico opened his mouth to argue, expecting to see the same indignant expression he'd seen at the wedding, the last time she reacted this way. The color had drained from her face, turning her so pale her skin nearly matched the white blond of her hair. Her eyes were pale, too, as though she were struggling to keep fear from invading their depths.

If he didn't know better, he'd say she seen a ghost.

What had he done? Or had something else happened in Boston, something more than the paparazzi trapping her in her home?

She blinked and the expression disappeared. Back was the Louisa he knew best. Distant and guarded. "It was wrong of me to lean on you like that," she said. "I lost myself for a second. It won't happen again."

"There's nothing wrong with turning to a friend when you're upset." He wondered if the word *friend* sounded as wrong to her ears as it did his. Surely holding a friend didn't feel as good as holding Louisa did. There was an amazing rightness in the way her body connected with his.

"I know, but…" She looked past him, to the window that looked into the front office. Inside, Vitale and Mario could be seen talking. "You've already done enough, letting me hide here."

That wasn't what she was going to say. She was worried what others would think.

"You are not hiding; you are working. Believe me, it is you who will be doing me the favor."

"Do you invite all your employees to stay at your house?"

"Only the beautiful ones," he teased. When she didn't share the joke, he turned serious. "No one will know that you're staying at my house."

"You don't think they'll figure it out?"

"Only if we tell them," he replied. "I've never had much taste for airing personal business in public."

Finally, she smiled. "Nico Amatucci, the model of discretion."

"Something like that."

"Just in case, now that I am working here, I think it's important that you treat me the same as any other employee. Especially considering today's headlines. No sense feeding the gossip."

"You're right." A voice in his head, though, told him gossip was only part of her reason. There was something more to her distance. And not the need to spend time alone, as she'd claimed the other day. It was as if she feared the attraction simmering between them. He supposed he couldn't blame her; the desire was stronger than anything he'd experienced before, as well.

"A regular employee," he said, echoing her words. Now was not the time to push for more. "I'll leave the hugs to your female friends. Speaking of, have you spoken to Dani?"

Louisa shook her head. "Not yet."

"Why not?" *Of course.* The way she looked away said everything. She was embarrassed. In spite of his lecture yesterday, she still worried her friends thought less of her.

If I had friends. Her comment from earlier came rushing back, and his insides tensed with anger on her behalf.

"You should call her," he said. "She's worried."

"I will. After I've settled in."

"Good." If she didn't, he would tell Dani and the others to come visit. She needed to know she had friends on her side, that the people of Monte Calanetti cared what happened to her.

As much as he did.

They spent the rest of the morning touring the winery. Nico explained the entire winemaking process from when the lifts brought freshly picked fruit to the loading dock to the fermentation stage, when the wine aged in oak barrels, just as it had for hundreds of years.

Occasionally, they passed an employee who would murmur a quick hello and rush away. While Louisa pretended not to mind the chilly reception, the words *if I had friends* repeated in his head. All he could picture was her barricaded in her house, surrounded by garbage she was too afraid to take outside while the world stared at her in judgment. He refused to let that happen again, not while she was under his protection.

By the time they finished and she was settled in the rear office with a stack of orders that needed fulfilling, his anger was at the boiling point. He marched back into the processing room and straight toward Mario and Vitale. "You will be friendly and polite to Louisa," he growled. "Is that clear?"

Both men nodded rapidly. He never raised his voice unless trying to yell over the machinery. "Good. You let the rest of the company know, as well. If I hear of anyone showing her disrespect, they will answer to me personally."

The people of Monte Calanetti would warm up to Louisa, even if he had to make them.

CHAPTER FIVE

"I DON'T BELIEVE IT. You really *are* working here."

Louisa froze in her chair at the sight of Marianna, Nico's sister, standing in the doorway wearing a decidedly vexed expression. "When Dani told me, I thought she was joking," she said.

Dani worked fast. Louisa had only called her best friend a few hours ago. Clearly the youngest Amatucci had rushed right over the second she got the news.

"It's only a temporary arrangement," she said. She managed to keep the defensiveness out of her voice, Barely. "I'm helping with order fulfillment."

The brunette waved away the answer as she stepped into the room. Being in her third trimester, her pregnant belly entered a full step before her. "He better not be making you work for a free dinner the way he used to make me. I don't care how wonderful a chef Rafe is, he's not as good as euros in your pocket."

She wanted Louisa to get paid? That was her concern? Louisa didn't know what to say. "You mean you don't mind my being here?"

"Why should I?" She eased herself into a nearby chair with a sigh. "Oh," she said seeing Louisa's expression. "You mean because the press said you two were dating."

"Among other things."

Again, the woman waved her off. "Who believes anything the newspapers say? Are those wine orders?" She motioned to a spreadsheet of names and addresses on the desk.

"Yesterday's telephone orders." Louisa grabbed the change of topic with more gratitude than she thought possible. "I haven't printed out the internet orders yet."

"Wow, Nico wasn't kidding when he said the business was doing well."

No, he wasn't. Wine vendors, restaurants, tourists—everyone was eager to stock Amatucci Red. "No surprise," Nico had remarked, winking in her direction. "Once they have a taste, they want more."

Louisa had poured herself a glass before bed last night, and it was as delicious as she remembered. *When it had been a lingering flavor in Nico's kiss*, she recalled with a shiver. Between the wine and yesterday's embrace, it was no wonder she'd dreamt of him all night.

Once they have a taste, they want more.

"At this rate he won't have much stock left for the

harvest festival," Marianna said, dragging Louisa back to the conversation at hand. "Unless he bottles more."

"I don't think the next vintage is ready." As Nico explained yesterday, the liquid needed to ferment at least five years before it was considered ready for bottling. "He said something about relabeling the remaining stock as Amatucci reserve."

"Relabeling and jacking up the price to reflect the reduced supply," Marianna mused aloud. "An old winemaker's trick, although few pull it off as well as my brother does. There's a reason he's won the country's Winemaker of the Year two years in a row."

"He has?"

"You didn't know?"

"No." She'd had no idea. "I knew the winery was successful." The sheer scope of his operations said as much. "But I didn't know how much so."

"Much as we tease him, my big brother has done very well with our family business. He's considered one of Italy's brightest wine stars."

"Careful, Marianna. Keep saying things like that and I'll believe you mean them." The subject of their conversation strolled in wearing a cocky grin. As Louisa had come to expect over the past couple of days, he already bore the evidence of hard work in the sun. The sight of his glistening biceps made her stomach flutter.

He nodded in her direction. "Although I hope you're suitably impressed."

"I am," she replied. "Very." Smug as the man was, the only awards he'd ever mentioned were the medals various vintages had won over the years, and those he attributed to the grapes, not to himself.

Now that she thought about it though, he didn't need to trumpet his accomplishments. His self-confidence said everything. "I was telling your sister that you planned to relabel the Amatucci Red," she said.

"Nothing wine lovers love more than to think they are getting something unique. And in this case they are."

He smiled again, straight at her this time, and Louisa found herself squeezing the arm of her chair. Who knew legs could give out while you were sitting? When he turned on the charm, it was all a person could do to keep her insides from turning to jelly. What her ex-husband could have done with magnetism like Nico's... *With a little charm, a man can sell anything*, Steven used to say.

Only Nico didn't just sell, he *made* wine. Good wine that he worked hard to produce. He came by his success honestly. That was what she found impressive.

Across the way, his baby sister offered a disdainful sniff. "Don't compliment him too much, Louisa. His head is big enough as it is."

"Not as big as your belly," Nico replied. "Are you supposed to be out in that condition?"

"You're as bad as my husband. I'm pregnant, not an invalid. I'm also bored stiff. Ryan is in Melbourne until tomorrow."

"So you came here looking for entertainment."

"Isn't that what big brothers are for?" the brunette asked, winking in Louisa's direction.

Louisa felt herself smile in return. Marianna's openness had her flummoxed. She was so certain she would be furious at her for involving Nico in her scandals. Yet here she was, joking as if none of the stories had ever happened.

"If you're going to stay, you're going to have to work," Nico told his sister.

"You want me to pick grapes?"

"No, we—" waving his arm, he indicated himself and Louisa "—can pick your brain. That is the reason I am here," he said. "We need to decide what the winery is going to do for the festival."

"You haven't decided yet?" Eyes wide, Marianna pushed herself straight. "Little last-minute, don't you think?"

"In case you haven't noticed, I've been busy. We still have time." He sounded confident, but Marianna rolled her eyes nonetheless.

"What kind of contribution are you talking about?" Louisa asked. More important, what did Nico expect from her?

"All the major businesses in Monte Calanetti are expected to build a float for the festival parade," Nico explained. "Something that celebrates the harvest or Tuscan heritage."

"Decorated with native foliage," Marianna added. "Grapes, olives, flowers."

"Wow." Louisa hadn't realized the festival was so elaborate. In her mind, she'd pictured a street fair similar to the St. Anthony's Feast in Boston's North End. "Sounds like a lot of fun."

"It is," Marianna told her. "Everyone works together to decorate and all the businesses compete to see who can outdo the others. The winner gets to display the harvest festival trophy. Amatucci Vineyards came in second last year. We created a miniature version of the plaza, complete with a working fountain." Pulling out her phone, the woman tapped a few buttons before turning the screen toward Louisa. "See?"

The photo showed Nico standing in front of the fountain, hands upon his hips. His smile dripping with pride. He looked like a superhero.

"Impressive," she murmured. Bet whoever took home the trophy didn't look nearly as good.

Marianna assumed Louisa meant the float. "Well, we started planning early. It's nearly impossible to assemble a prize-winning contribution at the last minute."

"Nearly, but not completely impossible," Nico retorted. "All we need is a good idea."

"Don't forget time," Marianna added.

Her brother waved her off, the same wave, Louisa noticed, his sister had used when dismissing the newspaper articles. "We will keep the design simple. It's not about being complicated, it's about being memorable. Like an Amatucci vintage."

His sister rolled her eyes again as Louisa stifled a snort. She was beginning to think some of his audacious behavior was on purpose. To see what kind of reaction he could elicit.

As far as the parade float went, however, he might have a point. She tried to remember the New Year's parades she used to watch on television as a kid. Most of the floats were a blur of colors. "Is there a theme?" she asked.

"Oh, there's always a theme," Nico replied. "But no one pays attention."

"No one meaning Ni—"

All of a sudden, Marianna gasped and clutched her stomach. Louisa and Nico were on their feet in a flash. The brunette held up a hand. "No need to panic. The baby kicked extra hard, is all. Going to be a little football player, I think. Uncle Nico is going to have to practice his footwork." Her face radiating maternal tranquility, she rubbed her swollen stomach. "Are you ready to play coach, Uncle Nico?"

Louisa's heart squeezed a little as the image of Nico and a miniature version of himself chasing a soccer ball popped into her head.

"I'm not sure I'd be the best coach," Nico replied. It was an uncharacteristically humble comment.

"I suppose you'd be happier if he or she wants to pick grapes."

"I—I just think we shouldn't be making plans for the child's future yet. It's too early. You don't want to court bad luck."

Funny, Louisa wouldn't have pegged Nico as the superstitious type. She supposed it came from being a farmer. No counting on the harvest until it happens or something like that.

Marianna acknowledged his reluctance with a frown. "Fine," she said. "We'll wait until he or she is born before making plans.

"Although I still think she's going to be a football player," she said under her breath.

They brainstormed ideas for a while, until a problem in the wine cellar drew Nico away. Louisa and Marianna continued for a little while longer, but it was obvious the pregnant woman was beginning to tire, despite her protests.

"Story of my life," Marianna said with a yawn. "I can't do anything for more than a half hour before needing a nap."

"Might as well enjoy it while you can," Louisa

told her. "Who knows when you'll get this much sleep again?"

The brunette nodded as if she'd delivered some great wisdom. "So true. I'll call you tomorrow and we can talk more about the project."

The two women walked to the front door. As usual, the few employees in the production area watched as they passed by. Marianna waved to each one with a smile while Louisa tucked her hair behind her ear and tried to act nonchalant. The past hour, watching Nico and his sister tease each other back and forth, had been the most relaxed she'd felt in forty-eight hours. She hated the idea that as soon as Marianna left, the atmosphere would go back to being tense and awkward.

They'd reached the door to the front office when Marianna suddenly turned serious. "May I ask you a question?" she asked.

Louisa's stomach tensed. Things had been going so well. What would change Marianna's mood so abruptly? It didn't help to see the other woman looking over her shoulder for potential eavesdroppers. "Of course," she said. "Anything."

"Is it me, or was Nico strangely disinterested when we were talking about the baby?"

Now that she mentioned it, Nico's reaction had been odd, especially considering how invested he had been when Marianna had first announced her pregnancy. Of course, at the time Marianna and her husband had been estranged and he had been worried about his sister's future. "You heard him; he doesn't want to court bad luck," she said.

"I know, but he's never been superstitious before," Marianna replied with a frown. "If anything, I'd expect him to tell me superstition was a bunch of nonsense. He used to hate it whenever our mother saw one of her omens."

"Your mother saw omens?"

"Oh, all the time. Usually after a fight with my father telling her they should make up."

Interesting. "Well, this is the first baby in the Amatucci family. Maybe it's making him tap into his roots."

"Maybe. He does like tradition."

"Plus, he's probably distracted. He has been super busy, between harvest and helping the town get ready for the festival." *And finding time to help her.*

"That is true. He does seem more distracted than usual these days." Marianna's frown quickly turned into a smile that was disarmingly similar to her brother's. "At least some of those distractions are good distractions, no?"

She didn't think that Louisa and he... The brunette's eyes sparkled, causing Louisa's stomach to tumble. "You said you didn't believe the papers."

"Oh, I don't believe the stuff about Luscious Louisa, but you and Nico... I saw that photo of the two of you dancing." She nudged Louisa's shoulder. *"Molto romantico."*

"It was just the camera angle," Louisa said, shaking her head. "The two of us are just friends."

"Friends, eh? Did he really throw a photographer off your balcony?"

Louisa sighed. "Yes, but again, it's not what you think. He was helping me out. You know your brother. If there's a situation that needs handling, he automatically takes charge."

"Hmm. I do know my brother," Marianna said with an odd smile.

"What does that mean?"

"Nothing. You are completely right. My brother does like to take charge. And in this case, I couldn't be happier."

Meaning she still thought they were involved. Louisa would have to have Nico set his sister straight. Still, it was nice to know her friend didn't think Louisa was out to seduce Nico for his money. Her trust meant a lot.

"You really don't care about what they said about me…about what happened in Boston? What they implied I was doing here in town?"

"Don't be silly. You're not responsible for what your ex-husband did. And you're the last person I'd call a temptress. I mean, look at what you're wearing…" She gestured at Louisa's jeans and green cotton sweater. "I'm dressed more seductively."

"It's the stiletto heels. They make everything seductive." Louisa tried to punctuate the remark with a laugh, but tears sprang to her eyes anyway. Marianna would never know how much her faith meant. Unable to form the words, she threw her arms around the pregnant woman's neck.

"Don't you know you're not supposed to get teary around a pregnant woman? My hormones won't be able to take it and I'll start crying, too." The young woman squeezed her tight, then released her with a watery grin. "I'll call you tomorrow."

Wiping her own eyes, Louisa nodded. "Do you mind if I don't walk you any farther? There might be reporters hiding across the street."

"Of course, I understand. And Louisa?" The brunette reached out to squeeze Louisa's hand. "I'm glad you and my brother are such good friends. He doesn't have that many."

Not many friends? "You're kidding right? We are talking about the same Nico Amatucci, aren't we?" The man with charisma to spare.

"Those are acquaintances, not real friends. He doesn't open himself up to many people. That makes you special."

Special. Right. Marianna's hormones were definitely out of whack.

A sound caught her attention. Looking across the

room, she spied Nico talking to an employee by the wine cellar doorway. Almost as if he knew she was thinking about him, he stopped what he was doing to look in her direction. He smiled and, for a moment, Louisa swore the entire winery tipped on its axis. *That makes you special...*

Apparently, Marianna wasn't the only one out of whack.

Louisa was upstairs asleep when Nico got home. He'd planned it that way. Following their embrace the day before, he decided it made sense for them to keep as much distance as possible, so he made a point of working as late as possible, along with heading into the fields before sunrise. The idea was for the long hours to make him too tired to remember the way her body had fit against his, allowing him to sleep without disturbance.

He didn't count on Marianna stopping by and stirring up other disturbing thoughts.

His sister was having a baby, he thought as he poured a glass of Chianti. Despite knowing this for months, it hadn't truly dawned on him until she'd called him Uncle Nico that she was starting a family of her own. Both she and his brother, Angelo, were moving forward with their lives, while here he was in the ancestral home maintaining the past. He, who was so determined never to repeat the madness of his parents.

Settling back on the sofa, he stared in the dim light at the dark square of the unlit fireplace. In his head, he could hear the sound of his parents laughing and clinking glasses. When they were happy, they laughed a lot, but when they stopped laughing… At least his father stayed in nice hotels when Mama threw him out.

All highs and lows, Carlos used to say. *No in betweens*. He never understood how that worked. How people could go from hot to cold to hot again in the blink of an eye. He once told Floriana that it was one thing to have passion in the bedroom, but it was quite another to have passion rule your life. Right before Floriana left, she told him that he had no passion, period.

She'd made a strong argument. He'd barely blinked when she'd said it.

He wondered what she would have said if she'd seen him throw that photographer off the balcony? Probably that she didn't recognize him. Again, she would have a point; Nico barely recognized himself the past couple of days, he was behaving so out of character.

Maybe Louisa really was a siren like the tabloids said. The thought made him chuckle into his glass.

"Nico? Is that you?"

The object of his thoughts appeared at the top of the stairs, a backlit silhouette. It took about two seconds for Nico to become aroused. Another thing that was out of character for him was how he couldn't seem to stop wanting her. Usually, when a woman said she wasn't interested, he moved on. No sense knocking on a door that wouldn't open. With Louisa, however, he didn't want to just knock, he wanted to kick the door in.

"Sorry to wake you," he said. "I was just having a glass of wine before bed."

"Long day?"

"Harvest takes a lot of preparation. Did Mario get you home all right?" He'd ordered his intern to escort her in case there were photographers lying in wait.

"He did. I hope you don't mind, but I got hungry and made some dinner. Puttanesca. There are leftovers in the fridge."

The notion of her at home in his kitchen caused a curious end-over-end sensation in the center of his chest. "Thank you."

"No problem. Good night," she said. Her silhouette hesitated. "Will I see you at breakfast?"

He thought of how good she looked drinking espresso across from him, and the sensation repeated itself. "Afraid not. I have to be in the fields early."

"Oh. Okay. I'll see you at the winery then."

Any disappointment he heard in her voice was pure imagination. As he finished his Chianti, he made a note to take the newspapers with him again when he left tomorrow. The "Royal Wedding Scandal," as they were calling it now, continued to dominate the tabloids, and he wanted to protect Louisa from the exposure.

Is that the argument you're using? Not that you don't want her leaving town? The very thought of her getting on the bus made his heart seize.

Out of character indeed.

The newspapers were missing again. For the second day in a row, Louisa came down for breakfast to discover both Nico and the papers gone from the house.

Who did he think he was, censoring her reading material?

She tracked him down in the fields and asked him that exact question.

"Keep your voice down, *bella mia*," he replied. "Unless you want people to know about our living arrangement." He nodded down the row where a pair of farm hands were watching them with curiosity. "And to answer your question, I wasn't aware I was 'censoring' anything."

"Then where are the newspapers?"

"I took them with me to read over coffee."

"Read about the Royal Wedding Scandal, you mean."

"Where did you hear about that?" The mask of indifference he'd been wearing slipped, proving his deception. Louisa glared at him. "Princess Christina called me this morning to ask how I was doing. She wanted me to know she and Prince Antonio didn't care what people were saying."

"See? Didn't I tell you that your friends would stand by you?"

Yes, he had, and Christina's phone call had meant more to her than she could say. That wasn't the point at the moment, however. "Don't try to change the topic. This is about you keeping information from me."

Nico sighed. "I was trying to protect you from useless gossip."

"Useless or not, you don't have the right to decide what I read and what I don't read." She rubbed her arms. Despite the sun beating down, her skin had turned to gooseflesh. She felt as though she'd had this conversation before with Steven. Only then the argument had been in her head because she'd not dared to speak her mind. Today was the first time she'd said the words aloud.

"I'm sorry. You were so upset by the headlines the other morning, I wanted to save you further distress." While talking, he pulled a grape off the vine and crushed it between his fingers. "I hate seeing you sad," he added, staring at his stained fingers.

The sweetness behind his answer dispelled a little of her anger. Only a little, however. "That's not your call to make, Nico. It's not your job to protect me from the headlines."

"No, just the paparazzi," he replied.

Louisa winced. He had her there. She was using him for protection, making her indignation over the newspapers sound more than a little hypocritical. "Do you want me to move back to the palazzo?"

"Do you want to move back?"

She toed the dirt with her sandal. Short answer? No. She liked having him nearby. Which meant maybe she should move back. "I don't know."

"Oh." He grabbed his satchel, which sat on the ground by his feet, and headed down the row.

She followed him. Thankfully the workers had moved to another row, leaving them in privacy. "That's all you're going to say?"

"You're not a prisoner, Louisa. You can do whatever you want."

Though cool, she could still hear the hint of hurt in his voice. Problem was, what she wanted scared her. She wanted the security she felt when she was wrapped in Nico's arms. *Which is exactly the opposite of why you came to Italy in the first place. What happened to standing on your own two feet for a change?*

"So what did the headlines say anyway?" she asked.

"You mean you didn't go online and look?"

"No." Her cheeks burned. Going online would

have been the easy solution, but she'd been too busy being indignant to turn on the computer. "I came looking for you instead."

"Well, you didn't miss much," Nico replied.

"Apparently I did, or you wouldn't have taken the papers." And he wouldn't be studying the Sangiovese leaves so intently. The winemaker had two very distinct stares, she'd come to realize. His intense "never missed a beat" stare that made her skin tingle, and his "I'm not telling you the whole story so I'm going to look at something else" stare. "Tell me."

"No doubt Christina told you about the royal wedding part. Halencia's government is afraid you might try to entice the royal family into making dubious investments."

"She told me." That wasn't the whole story, though. Not based on how Nico continued to stare at the vines. He took a deep breath. "They also interviewed my former fiancée."

CHAPTER SIX

"OH." IT WAS not the answer Louisa expected. She had suspected the papers would continue plumbing their erstwhile romance, but, in her self-involved haze, she hadn't thought about them digging into Nico's past. Dozens of questions came to mind, but the only words she could manage to say out loud were "I didn't realize you'd been engaged."

He shrugged. "It was a long time ago."

But not so long ago the memory didn't bother him. "Did she say something bad?" Was that why he continued to avoid her eyes?

"Actually she was surprisingly diplomatic. But then, Floriana was—is—a very good person."

If she was so good, why then why was she an ex? Louisa tried to picture the kind of woman Nico would propose to. Someone beautiful, no doubt. And smart. She would have to be smart to keep up with him. More questions came to mind, like what had kept them from the altar? From the shadows filling his expression, the decision hadn't been his, at least not completely.

Her annoyance from before all but forgotten, she reached out to touch his arm. "I'm sorry if it dredged up a lot of bad memories."

At last, he shifted his gaze, turning from the grapes to where her fingers rested on his forearm. As always happened, when his eyes fell on her, the attention made her body tingle. "Not everyone is made to get married."

True or not, his answer, with its lonely, resigned tone, hurt her to hear. Louisa found it hard to think of Nico as ever being lonely—the concepts *Nico* and *alone* seemed like polar opposites. But lines had suddenly appeared around his mouth and eyes as he spoke, lines that could only be etched from sadness.

"Sometimes we just pick the wrong person the first time around, is all," she said, thinking of her own mistake.

"Sometimes. I should check the Brix content on these vines." Pulling away from her touch, he reached for his satchel.

He didn't want to talk about it. Fine. If anyone understood the need to bury past mistakes, she did, and if changing topics took the sadness away from his eyes, all the better.

Nico wasn't the only one who hated to see another person sad.

"Are they ready for harvest?" she asked.

"You tell me." Picking a grape, he pressed it to her lips. Louisa could taste the sweetness the moment she bit down. Once she moved past the feel of his fingers on her lips, that is. "Mmm, delicious."

"If the sugar content matches up, I'll tell the foreman to have his team start working this field tomorrow. By the time we finish, the other fields, yours, should be ready."

"You mean they aren't all ready at the same time?" She stole another grape. The fruit was still sweet, but it didn't make her lips respond like the one he fed her had.

"Grapes on the northern side of the vineyard always ripen sooner. They're on a slope angled to get the most sun throughout the day. Carlos used to call Northern grapes *favorito della Natura* because they got the most sunshine."

"Nature's favorites?"

"He had names for all the fields. The ones in the southern field he called *scontroso*—grumpy— because they were often slow to ripen."

"Wouldn't you be grumpy, too, if the other field was the favorite?"

"That's what I used to tell him."

Louisa smiled, imagining the two men walking the rows, nicknaming the plants. "Carlos sounds like a character."

"He was a very wise man. A born winemaker."

Whose fields would be ruined, but for Nico's care. Guilt kicked at her conscience. If only she could have claimed her inheritance sooner. "I had no idea any of the Bertonellis ever existed," she said. "My mother never talked about my father's family." Never talked about her father, period, actually. Geoffrey Harrison was a smooth-talking liar best left unmentioned.

"Don't feel bad. I never knew he had relatives in America."

"Tight family bonds, huh?" she said. The sarcasm came out more bitter than she meant.

"Trust me, family bonds aren't always so wonderful. They can get in the way, too. Like baby sisters deciding you need to entertain them when they are pregnant and bored."

Who did he think he was kidding? He'd loved Marianna's visit yesterday and they both knew it.

"I would have killed for a brother or sister," she said. "Most of my life, it was just my mom and me. We used to joke it was us against the world."

"Must be upsetting for her to see her daughter being lambasted in the press. Have you talked to her?"

"No. She…um…" It was her turn to study the grape vines. How did she explain that she'd screwed up the one good relationship in her life? She'd love to blame Steven again, but this time she had only herself to blame. "I don't want to bother her."

Just as she recognized his evasion tactics, Nico recognized hers. "You don't think your mother's aware of what's going on?" he asked.

"I'm sure she is, but…" But Louisa was too embarrassed to call and talk about it. "The two of us were estranged for a while. I don't want to spoil things by bringing up bad news right as we're getting on better footing."

This wasn't the direction she planned for their conversation to take. Seemed as though whenever the two of them talked lately, she found herself sharing some facet of her past she'd sworn to keep secret. Frightening, how easily she exposed herself to him, more frightening than her desire to lean on his shoulder, and yet at the same time, the words tumbled out without pause.

Perhaps it was because Nico accepted what she said without pushing for more. Like now, he simply nodded and, hands in his back pockets, began sauntering down the row. Made her feel, in spite of how easily the information came out, that she was in control of the information she chose to share.

Mimicking his posture, Louisa headed after him, and the two of them walked in silence for several feet.

"Carlos taught me to appreciate the art of wine-making," he said after a moment, returning to their earlier conversation. Again, Louisa silently thanked him for not pushing. "He never let me forget that ours is a centuries-old craft, and as such we have an obligation to make the best wine possible."

"And your father? He was a vintner, too, was he not?" Strange that Nico's allegiance would be to his neighbor and not the man who raised him. "Did Carlos teach him, as well?"

"My father made wine, but not like Carlos. He was, shall we say, too distracted by other things."

Distracted how? Dying to know, Louisa had to bite her tongue to keep from asking. After all, she owed Nico the same courtesy he showed her when it came to privacy.

He answered anyway. "My mother, for one thing. Women who weren't my mother, for another. Don't worry," he added before she could offer sympathy. "Mama gives as good as she gets."

"They're still together?" She didn't know why that surprised her, but it did.

"They have what you would call a fiery relationship," Nico replied. "They've separated and reunited more times than I can count, swearing to God every time that they cannot live without each other, and they can't, for about a year or so. Then the plates begin to fly again." The early-morning sun caught his eyes as he cocked his head. Even when sad, he was beautiful. "You could practically hear the clock ticking between breakups."

"I'm sorry."

"Why are you apologizing? You didn't do anything."

No, but she felt as though she needed to say *something*. She knew that feeling of heavy expectancy all too well, the horrible sense of foreboding as you waited—and waited—for some undefined disaster to strike. "Is that how you ended up at the palazzo?"

"The palazzo vineyards were my escape. No chaos, no drama. Just peace and quiet." He took a long, deep breath, making Louisa wonder if he wasn't trying to internalize those very same qualities now. "At first I just went and watched the workers. Then one day Carlos came by—I think the workers told him about me—and he understood.

"My parents' reputations were well-known," he added with a smile. "Anyway, after that, he said if I was going to spend time in the vineyards, I was going to learn about them."

"You're very lucky," Louisa said. How often had she wished she had an ally like Carlos, only to end up hating herself because her isolation was no one's fault but her own?

"I know."

It dawned on her that Carlos Bertonelli had rescued them both, albeit in different ways. Shame rolled through her as she thought about how long it had taken her to claim her inheritance. She'd nearly let her sanctuary fall to pieces because she'd foolishly let herself be convinced there was no escaping her marriage.

"I'm sorry I never got to meet him," she said.

"Me, too." His lips curled into a smile. "He would have liked you a lot, you know," he told her. "The old man always had a soft spot for beautiful women. Right up to the end."

Louisa blushed at the compliment. "He must have loved Marianna, then."

"Of course he did. After his wife died, he would ask her to play the role of harvest queen. He used to tell people it was easier than choosing someone different each year, but everyone knew it was because he had a soft spot for her."

"There's a festival queen?"

"No one told you?"

"No." Although she could certainly picture the beautiful Marianna being selected as queen no matter her age.

"Oh yes, it's a tradition for the local nobility to lead the festivities." Nico told her. "If the nobleman wasn't married, then he would select a maiden from the village to act as his queen for the day. Although in those cases, I suspect there were a few other duties involved, as well." He grinned. "You seriously did not know?"

Louisa shook her head. The thing about Monte Calanetti's traditions running so deep was that everyone assumed they were common knowledge.

"It's not something that normally comes up in conversation," she said. "Who took over as the festival king after Carlos died?" The sunburn on Nico's cheeks grew a little darker. "Why am I not surprised?" She could only imagine the crowd clamoring to play his queen.

"Someone had to," he said. "Of course, now that you're here I will gladly abdicate the title."

She laughed. "Oh sure. People would love to see me lead the harvest parade. I can see the headlines now—Luscious Louisa Reigns from on High."

Why wasn't Nico laughing? Granted, it wasn't the funniest joke but he could at least smile at her attempt to make light of her problems. "Actually…" he began.

"You're joking." He was joking, right? "You're suggesting I play the role of harvest queen?"

"It's not a suggestion," he replied.

"Good."

"It's what's expected."

"Excuse me?" Did he say *expected*? The word ran down her back. She didn't do *expected* anymore.

"It's tradition," Nico continued. "As owner of Palazzo di Comparino, *you* are the local nobility. Therefore, people will expect you to take Carlos's place."

"No, they won't." Nico was the town nobility, she was merely notoriety.

"Yes, they will," he quickly retorted. "It's tradition."

Again with tradition. As if that justified everything. Who cared if it was tradition or not? Had he forgotten about the paparazzi, the whole reason she was hiding out at the vineyard? "I'm trying to avoid having my picture taken, remember? Not encourage the papers by parading down the middle of the street."

"You won't be encouraging anything. The festival isn't for another week. By that time, the scandal will have gone away," he said.

Says you. "Scandals never go away," she shot back. They were like weeds, going dormant only to crop up during another season. "People have long memories. Just because the headlines fade, doesn't mean they will have forgotten who I am. The people here aren't going to want to expose Monte Calanetti to ridicule."

An aggravated growl vibrated deep in Nico's throat. *"Madonna mia,"* he said, gesturing toward the heavens, "I thought we were past this. You have got to have faith in the people you live with."

"Oh sure, because the world has been so supportive up until now." She couldn't go through another round of sneers and whispers. She *wouldn't.*

"Monte Calanetti is not Boston."

"Maybe, maybe not," she said. That didn't matter.

"What's the big deal anyway? So I don't lead the parade. Traditions can change, you know. There's no law that says everything needs to stay exactly the same."

"I know," he spat.

Then why were they even having this foolish argument? He knew she wanted to stay under the radar. "Look, it's not just the risk of gossip," she told him. Why she was bothering to add to her argument, she didn't know, but she was. "Even if you're right, and people don't care about the headlines, I'm not living that kind of life again."

"What do you mean, 'that kind of life'?"

"The whole socialite thing. I played that role long enough when I was with Steven." She was done with plastic smiles and faking happiness. With being told when and where and how.

He frowned. "So you don't care that when Carlos passed on the palazzo, he passed along the responsibilities that came with it?"

"No, I don't." She'd come to Italy to live *her* life and no one was going to make her do anything different.

"I see," Nico said, nodding. "Now I understand."

"Do you?"

"*Si.* Comparino is merely a piece of property to you. No wonder you ignored its existence for so long."

Ignored? *Ignored?* Oh, did he just say the wrong thing. Louisa's vision flashed red. "Don't you dare," she snarled. "I didn't ignore anything. From the moment I opened the lawyer's letter, I wanted to be here." He had no idea how badly. How many nights she'd lain awake wishing she could board a plane and escape.

"Of course you did. Your desire to be here was obvious from all those months you left the place to ruin."

"I was testifying against my husband!"

Her shout sounded across the vineyard. If the field workers didn't know her business before, they certainly knew it now. Let them. By this point, the damn trial was public knowledge anyway. What was another mention? Taking a deep breath, she added in a lower voice. "I couldn't leave the country for an entire year."

The explanation might have been enough for some, but not Nico. Crossing his arms, he positioned himself in front of her, his broad shoulders blocking the path. "You ignored us for over *two* years, Louisa, not one," he reminded her. "Or did the authorities refuse to let you leave the country before the arrest, as well?"

Not the authorities. Damn it all. How had she ever let the conversation turn in this direction? To the one secret she hoped to never have to say aloud.

"It's complicated," she replied. It would be too

much to ask for Nico to continue accepting her terse answers at face value. Not this time. He was angry; he would want answers.

Sure enough, his eyes burned dark and intense as he stood, arms folded, waiting for her to continue. Louisa's skin burned from the intensity. She thought about lying, but she'd never been very good at it. Pretending, masking her emotions, sure, but out-and-out lies? Not so much. Looking back, it was a wonder she'd managed to keep Comparino a secret at all.

"I didn't have a choice—I had to stay in Boston. If Steven had known I had property in my name—property of my own—he would have..." Angry tears threatened. She looked down so he wouldn't see them.

"He would have what?" Nico asked.

"Taken it," she replied, choking on the words. "He would have taken the palazzo the same way he took everything else I had."

At last, the ugly truth was out in the open and Nico would never look at her the same way again. How could he? She was a stupid, gullible fool who let a master manipulator ruin her life. Shame rose like bile, sour and thick in her mouth. She didn't dare raise her eyes to look into his face. She couldn't bear to see pity where there'd once been admiration. There was only one thing she could do.

Spinning around, she took off down the path.

* * *

What the—? Nico stared at Louisa's retreating figure before sprinting after her. "Louisa, hold up!"

"Leave me alone," she said. "I have to get to the winery." She sounded as though—was she crying?

It didn't take long for him to close the distance between them. When he did, he touched her shoulder hoping to slow her pace, only to have her tear free of his grip so fiercely you'd think he was physically restraining her. She turned and snarled, "I said leave me alone."

She was crying. Tears streaked her cheeks. Their tracks might as well have been scratches on his skin, they hurt that much to see. This was about more than her thief of a husband stealing property. "What did that bastard do to you?"

"Nothing. It doesn't matter. Forget I said anything."

She tried to surge ahead again but he had height to his advantage. It was nothing for him to step ahead and block her path. Not unexpectedly, she shoved at his shoulder trying to make him move. "I said forget it."

"I can't," he said, standing firm. Not after seeing those tears. "Talk to me."

"Why? So you can laugh at what a stupid idiot I am?"

Idiot? Nico shook his head. "I could never think that of you."

"Then you're a bigger fool than I am," she said, jaw trembling. "And I'm... I'm..."

Her face started to crumble. "I'm a damn big one."

CHAPTER SEVEN

LOUISA BURIED HER face in her hands. Nico stood frozen by the sight of her shaking shoulders, wanting to comfort her but afraid his touch might make her run again. Eventually his need to hold her won out, and he wrapped her in his arms. She sagged into him, fists twisting into his shirt. His poor sweet Louisa. Steven Clark should be glad he was in prison because otherwise Nico would… Heaven knows what he would do. He pressed his lips to the top of her head and let her cry.

After a while, the shaking eased. "I'm sorry," she said, lifting her head. "I didn't mean to lose it like that. It's just sometimes I think, no matter how hard I try, Steven will always be there, taunting me. That I'll never completely escape him."

Suddenly all her comments about needing to be on her own took on new meaning. She was running from more than scandal and a failed marriage, wasn't she? He could kick himself for not realizing it sooner. He risked another brush of his lips against her hair before asking, "Did he hurt you badly?"

"You mean physically?" She shook her head. "He never laid a hand on me."

Thank God. Not all abuse was physical, however. Emotional abuse was insidious and painful in its own way. His parents played mind games all the time, driving one another to madness out of revenge or jealousy. "But he hurt you all the same, didn't he?"

"Yeah, he did," she said, giving a long sigh. Backing out of his embrace, she stumbled just far enough to be out of reach, wiping her tears as she walked. "It's my fault, really. The signs were all there from the very beginning, but I chose to ignore them. Love makes you stupid."

"He was also an accomplished liar," he reminded her, his nerves bristling when she mentioned the word *love*. From everything he'd heard of the man so far, Steven Clark didn't deserve Louisa's affection, and he certainly didn't deserve her self-recrimination.

If his underlying message made it through, it wasn't evident in Louisa's answering sigh. "He certainly was. But he was also incredibly charming and romantic, and I was twenty-one years old."

"Barely an adult."

"True, but I was certain I knew everything."

"What twenty-one-year-old isn't?" he replied.

His attempt to lighten the moment failed. Tired of standing, and suspecting getting the entire story would take some time, Nico motioned for her to follow him a few feet ahead, to a small gap between plants. He sat down beneath the branches, the dirt cool and damp through his jeans, and patted the space beside him. Louisa hesitated for a moment before joining him.

"How did you meet him?" he asked when she finally settled herself. He told himself he was asking because he wanted to understand what happened, and not because of the burning sensation the man's name caused in his chest.

"At work. My first job out of college. I was so psyched when I got the job, too," she said, in a voice that still held lingering pride. "Clark Investments was the hottest business in the city at the time. Steven was a rock star in Boston financial circles."

A rock star with twenty years on his starry-eyed employee, Nico thought, gritting his teeth. "You must have been very good to get the job."

"I was."

There was such gratitude in her smile, as if it had been a long time since someone had acknowledged her abilities. Nico laid the blame at the feet of her ex-husband. "Anyway, I met Steven a couple months after I started—on the elevator of all places—and all I could think was *Steven Clark is talking to me.*

Later, he told me he was so impressed he had to ask me out."

That, thought Nico, might have been the most honest thing Steven Clark had ever said. What man with two eyes wouldn't be impressed by her?

"I felt like Cinderella. Here I was, a girl from a single-parent family in a blue-collar town while Steven was sophisticated and had experienced things I'd never dreamed of doing. Things like skiing in the Alps and diving with sharks." She scooped a handful of dirt and let it sift through her fingers. "I should have known then, the stories were too outrageous to be true, but like I said, love—"

"Makes you blind," he finished for her. Why that phrase bothered him so much, he didn't know. Of course she'd loved the man; he was her husband.

"He flew us to Chicago once because I said I liked deep dish pizza. Who wouldn't fall for a gesture like that?" she asked. "I thought I'd met Prince Charming.

"My friends didn't think so. They said he made them feel uncomfortable. Steven said it was because they were jealous."

"Perhaps they were."

"My mother, too?" she asked. "She didn't like him at all. Called him a slicker version of my father and said she didn't trust him."

That was why they were estranged. Nico could guess what happened. Her mother didn't approve, and Steven took advantage of the disagreement to push them further apart.

"We had this awful fight," she told him. "I accused her of not wanting me to be happy, that because she was alone and miserable, she wanted me to be alone and miserable, too. When I told Steven, he said, 'that's all right. I'm all the family you need now.'" The fresh tears in her eyes had Nico moving to take her in his arms again. She shook him off, getting to her feet instead. "I didn't talk to her for almost five years. She could have died and I wouldn't have known."

"That's not true." She was letting her guilty conscience color her thinking.

"Isn't it?" she replied, turning around. "Who would tell me? I cut myself off from everyone I used to know. Because they didn't fit with my new life."

And Nico could guess who had put that thought in her head. A chill ran through him as he slowly began to understand what she meant by Steven taking everything from her.

She'd turned away from him again, her face turned to the foliage. Nico could see her fingering the edge of one of the leaves. Her hands were shaking.

"You tell yourself you're too smart to fall for someone's lies," she said. "You read stories of women trapped in bad relationships and you can't understand how they can be so foolish. That is, until it happens to you."

"Louisa, don't…"

"Don't what? Blame myself? Tell the embarrassing truth?"

Don't tell me at all. Rising to his feet, Nico walked behind her and curled his hands atop her shoulders to steady her. There was no need for her to go on; he'd heard enough.

Unfortunately for both of them, Louisa had unsealed a bottle that insisted on being emptied because she immediately shook her head. "I think maybe I need to tell someone," she whispered. "Maybe if I say the words aloud…"

Nico could hear her breath rattle with nerves as she took a deep lungful of air before she began to speak. "When it first started, I barely noticed. When you're in love you're supposed to want to spend every minute with each other, right?"

"Yes," Nico replied. His hands were still on her shoulders, and it was all he could do not to pull her tight against him.

"And then, after we were married, when Steven suggested I stop working to avoid gossip, well that made sense, too. It was expected I would be with him at corporate dinner parties and charitable functions. Could hardly do that if I was working full-time."

Lots of women managed both, thought Nico.

Louisa could have, as well. But that would have meant having a life of her own, and it sounded as though having an independent wife was the last thing Steven Clark wanted.

He honestly could strangle the man. Here was one of the things that made Louisa such a treasure. Challenging her was exciting. If Nico had a woman like her in his life, he'd do everything in his power to aid in her success, not pin her down like some butterfly under glass. Steven Clark was an idiot as well as a thief.

"When did you realize…?"

"That I was trapped?"

"Yes." Actually, he hadn't known what he'd meant to ask, but her question was close enough.

"I skipped a charity planning committee to do some last-minute Christmas shopping. One of the other members told Steven, and he lost it. Demanded to know where I'd been all day and with whom." She pulled the leaf she'd been playing with from its branch, sending a rustling noise rippling down the row. "To this day I'm not sure what frightened me more. His demand or the fact there were people reporting my actions to him."

Neither aspect sounded very comfortable. "You stayed, however." Because she loved him.

"Where was I supposed to go? None of the assets were in my name. I'd alienated everyone I used to know, and Steven didn't have friends so much as business associates. I couldn't trust those people to help me, not when Steven was handling their money. I couldn't go anywhere. I couldn't talk to anyone. I was stuck."

The proverbial bird in a gilded cage, Nico thought sadly.

"Surely your mother or your friends…"

"And have to listen to them tell me how right they'd all been? I couldn't." Nico wanted to smile despite the sad situation. That was his American. Stubborn to the end, even when it hurt her.

"Discovering I'd inherited the palazzo was torture. Here I had this safe haven waiting for me, and I couldn't get to it. Even if by some miracle I did find a way to evade Steven's radar, with his money and connections, he would have eventually tracked me down."

The leaf she'd been holding fluttered to the ground as she sighed. "In the end it was easier to go along to get along."

"You mean accept the abuse," Nico said.

"I told you, it wasn't abuse."

They both knew she was lying. Steven might not have hit her or yelled insults, but he'd abused her in his own despicable way. He'd stolen her innocence and her freedom and so much more. Nico could feel the anger spreading through him. If it was possible to kill a man by thoughts alone, Steven Clark would be dead a thousand times over.

Arms hugging her body, Louisa turned to look at him with cavernous eyes, the white-blond curtain of her hair casting her cheeks with shadows.

"The day I stumbled across those financial reports was the best day of my life, because I knew I could finally walk away," she said.

Only walking away hadn't been as easy as she made it sound.

The truth wasn't as simple as she described. Walking away was never easy. The details didn't matter. Her story explained a lot, however. Why she balked every time he offered to help, for example. It definitely explained why she feared her friends would cut her off.

"Do you still love him?" It was none of his business, and yet he could not stop thinking about her words before. Love makes you blind.

"No. Not even in the slightest."

If he shouldn't have asked the question, then he should definitely not have felt relief at her answer. He did, though. To save her heart from further pain, that was all.

"I'm sorry," he said.

"I told you before, I don't want your pity."

Her voice was rough from crying, the raw sound making him hate Steven Clark all the more. "I don't pity you," he told her truthfully. He didn't. He *ad-*

mired her. Did he know what kind of strength it took to pull herself free from the hell she had become trapped in? Not only pull herself free, but to begin again?

"What I meant was that I am sorry I accused you of abandoning the palazzo," he said.

"Oh." The tiniest of blushes tinged her cheekbones as she looked down at her feet. "Thank you," she said. "And I'm sorry I lost my temper."

"Then we are even." Funny, but he'd forgotten why she'd lost her temper in the first place.

By silent agreement, they started walking toward the production facilities. They'd been in the field most of the morning, Nico realized, or so said the sun beating on the back of his neck. His employees would be looking for him. Wasn't like him to ignore the winery for so long. Add another uncharacteristic behavior to the growing list.

Even though Louisa's confession answered a lot of questions, Nico found his mind more jumbled than before. Mostly with vague unformed ideas he couldn't articulate. Finally, because he felt the need to say *something* while they walked, he said in a quiet voice. "I'm glad you made it to Italy."

The sentiment didn't come close to capturing any of the thoughts swirling in his head, what he wanted to say, but it was enough to make Louisa smile.

"Are you really?" she asked.

She sounded so disbelieving.

"Yes, really," he replied. More than he'd realized until this moment. The town wouldn't be the same without her. The palazzo and Monte Calanetti needed her. He…

The thought lingered just out of reach.

He knew he was taking a risk, but he closed the distance between them anyway, reaching up with his hands to cradle her face. "I can't imagine Monte Calanetti without you."

Her trembling lower lip begged for reassurance or was it that he begged to reassure her? To kiss her and let her know just how glad he was to have her in Monte Calanetti.

Cool fingers encircled his wrists, holding him. Stopping him. She was backing away yet again. "Thank you," she said, slipping free.

This time when she began to walk, Nico purposely lagged behind.

CHAPTER EIGHT

"MAY I BORROW you for a moment?"

Louisa was in the middle of attaching mailing labels to boxes when Nico appeared in her doorway. As soon as she looked in his direction, her stomach somersaulted. She blamed it on the fact that he'd startled her.

Along with the fact he looked as handsome as sin in his faded work clothes. How did the man do it? Look so perfect after being out in the fields for hours. None of the other workers wore hard labor as well. Of course there was always the chance he was supervising more than actually working, but standing around didn't seem his style. More likely Mother Nature wanted to make sure Nico looked a cut above all the rest.

Mother Nature did her job well.

Nico arched his eyebrow, and she realized he was waiting for a response. What had he asked? Right. To borrow her. "Sure," she replied. "What do you need?"

"Follow me to the lab."

Louisa did what he asked, her heart pounding in her chest. She couldn't blame being startled this time. Your palms didn't sweat when you were startled.

It'd been two days since their conversation in the vineyard, or rather since Louisa had bared her soul regarding her marriage. They hadn't talked since. Nico continued to leave the house before breakfast and didn't return until late. To be honest, Louisa wasn't sure he came home at all. After all, the dinner plate she left last night hadn't been touched. If it wasn't harvest season, she'd worry he was purposely avoiding her.

Oh, who was she kidding? She still worried, just as she was worried how to behave around him now. Strangely enough, however, it wasn't her meltdown—or her confession—that had her feeling awkward. It was the memory of Nico holding her close yet again.

Since arriving in Italy, Louisa could count on three fingers the number of times she'd truly felt safe and secure. All three had been in Nico's arms, and they were as engrained in her memory as any event could be. If she concentrated, she could feel his breath as it had brushed her lips when he'd said he couldn't imagine Monte Calanetti without her. The simplest of words, but they made her feel more special than she'd felt in a long time. With his touch gentle and sure on her cheeks, she'd wanted so badly for him to kiss her.

Still, the last time a man had made her feel special, she'd wound up making the biggest mistake of her life, and while she might be older and wiser, she was also a woman with desires that had been neglected for a long time. The idea of giving herself over to Nico's care left a warm fluttery sensation in the pit of her stomach—a dangerous feeling, to say the least. Thank goodness she managed to keep her head.

Thank goodness, too, that Nico understood. In fact, seeing his relaxed expression, she'd say he'd managed to brush the moment aside without problem.

Louisa was glad for that. Truly.

Nico's "lab" was located at the rear of the building a stone's throw from where the grapes were stored after being picked. Now that harvesting had begun, the rolling door that led to the loading dock was left permanently open so that the forklifts could transport the containers of grapes from the field trucks to the washing area. Louisa breathed deep, taking in as much of the sweet aroma as she could.

"Do you mind if I close the door?" Nico hollered. "It'll be easier to hear each other."

She shook her head. Out here the sound was much louder than by her office, where the machines were still dormant.

There was a click and the decibel level was suddenly reduced by half. "Much better," Nico said.

Better was relative. In addition to being small, the room was stuffed with equipment making the close space tighter still. Standing near the door, Louisa found herself less than a yard away from Nico's desk, and even closer to Nico himself. He smelled like grapes. To her chagrin, the aroma made her stomach flip-flop again.

Trying to look casual, she leaned against the door, arms folded across her midsection. "What is it you needed to talk about?" she asked him.

"Not talk. Taste."

He pointed to the equipment on his worktable. "I need a second opinion regarding this year's blend."

"This year's blend?" She knew that super Tuscans were wines made by combining different varieties of grape, but she assumed that once the formula was created, the blend stayed the same.

"Every harvest is different," Nico replied. "Sometimes only subtly, but enough that the formula should be tweaked. Mario and I have been playing with percentages all day, but we're not quite sure we've achieved the right balance."

"I see." Speaking of the university student, she didn't see him.

Nico must have seen her looking around because he said, "Mario has gone home. He was a little too enthusiastic a taster."

"You mean he got a little tipsy."

"Don't be silly. He needed a break, is all." He'd gotten tipsy. "Anyway, I think I'm close, but I could use a fresh palate."

"Wouldn't you be better off asking someone else? I'm not much of a wine connoisseur." If he wanted to know about finish and undertones, she couldn't help him.

"You don't have to be," he told her. "You just have to know what you like."

Stepping to the worktable, he retrieved two beakers containing purple liquid and a pair of wineglasses. "Fancy bottle," Louisa joked.

"Good things come in odd glass containers," he joked back. He poured the contents from each into its own glass and set them on the edge of his desk. "Tell me which one of these wines you like better."

"That's it?"

"That's it."

Simple enough. Picking up the first glass, she paused. "Am I supposed to smell it before I drink?"

"Only if you want to."

Louisa didn't. Things like that were better left to someone like Nico who actually understood what they were looking for. "And do I spit or swallow?" She vaguely remembered there was supposed to be some kind of protocol.

"Drink like you would a regular glass of wine. If you normally spit…"

She returned his smirk. "Fine. I get the point."

The contents of the first glass tasted amazing. Sweet but not overly so with just enough tang to make it stay on your tongue. Delicious. "Mmm," she said, licking her lips.

She was about to declare the choice easy until she tasted the second glass and found it equally delicious. "You're kidding," she said, setting the glass down. "There's supposed to be a difference?"

"Don't focus on finding the difference. Tell me which one you like better."

She tasted each one again, this time with her eyes closed in order to really focus. Took a couple of sips, but in the end, the first glass won out. "This one," she said, finishing the glass with a satisfied sigh. "Definitely this one."

When she opened her eyes, she found Nico watching her with an unreadable expression. His jaw twitched with tension as if he was holding back a response. "Tha…" He cleared his throat. Nevertheless his voice remained rough. "Thank you."

"I hope I helped."

"Trust me, you helped me a great deal."

"Good." Their gazes stayed locked while they talked. Louisa never knew there could be so many different shades of brown. The entire color wheel could be seen in Nico's irises.

"Would you like some more?" she heard him ask. Wine. He meant more wine. Louisa blinked, sending everything back into perspective. "Better not," she said. "I'm not as practiced a wine taster as you are. Or are you purposely trying to send me home like Mario?"

Nico slapped a hand against his chest, mimicking horror. "Absolutely not. We're shorthanded tonight as it is."

The float-decorating party. It was Marianna's idea. With so many of the employees working long hours, she didn't think it fair to ask them to help decorate the winery float, as well, so she'd convinced a group of friends to do it instead. Louisa had been the first person she'd recruited.

It would be Louisa's first public appearance since the headlines broke.

"Maybe I will have another glass," she said reaching for the beaker.

Nico's hand immediately closed around her wrist, stopping her. "There is no need to be nervous," he said. "These are your friends."

"I know." What amazed her was how much she meant it. A week ago she'd have been a crumbling basket of nerves, but not so much now. Partly because the story was winding down.

And partly because the man next to her was scheduled to be there, as well. Her personal protector at the ready, his presence made being brave a lot easier.

After much back and forth, it was decided the

vineyard would have to give up on trying to win any awards and instead design as simple a float as possible. Something that could be assembled with minimal manpower in as short a time as possible. Nico was the one who came up with the idea. Some of the parts of last year's float, namely the fountain, were in storage. All they needed was fresh foliage. While it was too late in the day for the fountain to spout water again, they could easily recycle it into a different design. And so it was decided they would recreate the royal wedding. Two of his employees would play Prince Antonio and Princess Christina while others played wedding guests. The couples would waltz around the fountain, pretending to dance beneath the stars. It might not be an entirely accurate representation, but it would do the winery proud.

As she watched Nico and Mario retrieve the fountain later that afternoon, she couldn't help wondering if the idea reminded Nico of the kiss they'd shared. The one she'd told him to forget had ever happened. Which he apparently was having much better luck doing than she was.

Marianna's party attracted a crowd. In addition to Dani and Rafe, who came on their day off, there were several other couples Louisa had met at Marianna's baby shower and other events. There was Isabella Benson, one of the local schoolteachers, and her new husband, Connor, along with wedding planner Lindsay and her husband, Zach Reeves, who'd just returned from their honeymoon. Louisa chuckled to herself, remembering the jokes she and Nico had made at the royal wedding about Lindsay and Zach's obvious adoration for each other. Even Lucia Moretti-Cascini, the art expert who'd worked on the chapel restoration and who was in town visiting her in-laws, was there. Having appointed herself the unofficial design supervisor, she sat on a stack of crates with a sketch pad while swatting away suggestions from her husband, Logan. In fact, the only person missing was the organizer herself.

Not a single person mentioned the tabloid stories or Louisa's history in Boston. The women all greeted her with smiles and hugs, as if nothing had changed. After years of phony smiles and affection, their genuine embraces had her near tears. Only the reassuring solidity of Nico's hand, pressed against the small of her back, kept her from actually crying. "Told you so, *bella mia*," he whispered as he handed her a glass of wine.

In spite of Marianna's absence, the work went smoothly. In no time at all, the old pieces were in place and covered with a plastic skin, ready to be decorated.

Louisa and the other women were put in charge of attaching the foliage while the men assembled the foam cutouts that would make the frame for the palazzo walls.

"This is a first," Dani said as she pressed a grape into place.

"Hot gluing fruit to a chicken-wire nymph. Are we sure this is going to look like marble?"

"Lucia says it will, and she's the art expert," Louisa replied.

"Art expert. There aren't too many museums who deal with produce."

"They used grapes last year," Isabella reassured them, "and it looked wonderful."

"She's right. I saw pictures," Louisa said, remembering the photograph of Nico that Marianna had shown her. "Hopefully we'll do as good a job. I'd hate to embarrass the vineyard."

"I'm sure we won't, and if it does turn out a disaster, Nico can always keep it locked in the garage."

"True." Louisa reached for a grape to glue into place only to pick up her wineglass instead. Something had been nagging her since the party began and she needed Dani's perspective. "Did you know that as palazzo owner, I'm supposed to play the part of festival queen?" she asked as she took a drink.

"Really?"

"Nico told me it's a tradition."

Dani's eyes flashed with enthusiasm. "How exciting. Do you get to ride on the back of a convertible and wave to a crowd like a beauty queen and everything?"

"I have no idea." Although Dani had painted an

image she'd rather not contemplate. "I wasn't planning to do it at all."

"Why not, if it's tradition? Sounds like fun." Dani asked. "I always wanted to be the homecoming queen, but the title always went to some tall cheerleader type."

"I was a cheerleader."

Her friend took a sip of wine. "I rest my case."

"Hey, less drinking, more gluing," Isabella said, her dark head poking over the nymph's outstretched arm. "Do not make me come over there and take your wineglasses away."

Chastised, the pair ducked their heads, though Dani managed to sneak one more sip. "Seriously though," she said, reaching for the glue gun. "You should totally do it. You'd make a gorgeous festival queen."

"I'd rather be part of the crowd," Louisa replied. "I've had enough of the spotlight for one lifetime."

"That I can understand." Dani said, putting another grape in place. "I didn't want to bring up a sore subject, but how are you doing? You sound a lot better than you did when I spoke to you on the phone."

"I feel better," Louisa answered.

"You have no idea how worried I was when I saw those headlines. Rafe told me how brutal the paparazzi can be, and I was afraid one of them might try something scary."

"One did try," Louisa said, "but Nico scared him off."

"So I read in the papers. Thank goodness he showed up."

"Thank goodness is right." Not giving it a second thought, Louisa looked to the other side of the truck bed where he was arguing with Rafe over the foam placement. Sensing he was being watched, he looked over his shoulder and grinned.

She dipped her head before he could see how red her cheeks were. "I'm only sorry his help dragged him into the gossip pages, too," she said to Dani, hoping her friend didn't notice the blush either. "He's a good man."

"Rafe wouldn't be his friend if he wasn't," Dani replied. "I don't know if you've noticed, but my husband can be a little hard to please."

"A little?" Rafe Mancini's demanding reputation was legendary. He'd been known to toss vendors into the street for selling him what he considered subpar products.

And yet, the same chef and his wife had accepted Louisa without question. Louisa felt the swell of emotion in her throat again. Swallowing hard, she did her best to make her voice sound lighthearted "Have I told you I'm really glad we met on the bus from Florence?"

"Is this your not so subtle way of thanking me for being your friend?" Dani asked.

"Maybe."

Her fellow American gathered her in a hug. "I'm glad we're friends, too," she said. "Although if you get hot glue in my hair, I will kill you."

"And Lindsay and I will kill you both if you do not get to work," Isabella scolded. "We are not gluing all these grapes by ourselves."

"Jeez, I'm glad I'm not one of her students," Dani whispered.

"I heard that."

Louisa snorted, almost dropping the grape she was putting into place. The teasing reminded her of old times, when she and her college friends would get together and giggle over cocktails. Steven had hated that.

"You too, Louisa," Lindsay admonished. "Just because you're dating the boss doesn't mean you get to slack off."

Dating—? The newspaper photographs. Just when she thought she'd actually put them behind her. The only saving grace, if there could be one, was that at least these women didn't consider her some kind of financial predator. Like Marianna the other day, they saw it as a potential romance. "Nico and I aren't dating," she told them.

"Are you sure?" Isabella asked. "Those pictures—"

"Were pictures, that's all," she said, cutting her off. "The two of us are just friends."

"Sure, just like Zach and I are friends," Lindsay replied. She and Isabella exchanged smirks.

"Something tells me the lady protests too much," the teacher replied.

Louisa stared at the grape-covered plastic in front of her and reminded herself the women were only teasing. Nevertheless, that didn't stop her skin from feeling as if it was on fire. Not because she was embarrassed or ashamed, at least not in the way she expected to be. She was embarrassed because they were right.

She *was* protesting too much.

"I didn't realize you found the gluing of grapes so fascinating, my friend."

Nico did his best to look annoyed at his best friend, but the heat in his cheeks killed the effort. "Checking to see how much progress they are making, that is all."

"Not as much as there would be if you waited longer than thirty seconds between looks," Rafe replied.

He inclined his head to where the women were laughing and topping up their wineglasses. "It's all right, you know. She's a beautiful woman."

"Who? Your wife?"

"Of course, my wife. But I'm talking about Louisa. I saw the photograph of the two of you in the newspaper. Very romantic."

"We were at a wedding. Everything about weddings looks romantic."

"This was different. You were looking at her like…"

"Like what?"

"I don't know," his friend replied honestly. "I've never seen you look at a woman that way."

Perhaps because he'd never met a woman like Louisa before. "She's different," he said.

"Because she's an American. They have a different kind of energy about them. It's very…captivating."

Captivating was a good word. He felt as though he was under a spell at times, what with the uncharacteristic moods he'd been experiencing. He could feel his friend's eyes on him. "It's not what you think," he said.

"You aren't attracted to her?"

"Of course I am attracted. Have you looked at her?"

"Then it is exactly what I think. And, if that picture is to believed, the feeling is mutual. And yet the two of you…" His friend set down the foam block he was holding to give Nico a serious look. "You are not together. Since when do you not pursue an interested woman?"

"I told you, Louisa is different." Other women hadn't been traumatized by an emotionally abusive Prince Charming. "She's not the kind of woman you toy with."

"So don't toy."

Rafe made it sound so easy. Problem was Nico wasn't sure he could do anything else. "Not everyone is made for commitment like you are, my friend."

A warm hand clapped his shoulder. "What happened with Floriana was a long time ago. People change."

"Sometimes. Sometimes they don't." More often than not, they were like his parents, repeating the same mistakes over and over. With everything she'd been through, Louisa deserved better. "I've already broken the heart of one good woman," he said.

"And haven't you punished yourself enough for it?" His friend squeezed his shoulder. "You can't be afraid to try again."

Nico wasn't afraid, he was trying to be kind. Rafe meant well, but he didn't know everything. There were secrets Nico couldn't share with anyone.

Almost anyone, he amended, eyes looking at Louisa. He'd certainly shared about his parents.

It was a moot point anyway. "You are assuming the decision is 100 percent mine to make," he said. "Louisa is the one who is not interested. It was Louisa's choice to keep our relationship platonic." If she went through with selling the palazzo, they wouldn't even have that.

"That's too bad."

"Yes, it is." Why lie about his disappointment?

He watched as Louisa laughed with her friends. She had her hair pulled back, and there was purple staining her fingers. Beautiful. Seeing her relaxed made him happy.

"But," Nico said, "you can't force emotions." If anyone knew that, it was him.

His cell phone rang, saving him from any further rebuttals. "About time," he said as the caller ID popped onto the screen. "It's Ryan," he told Rafe. "You tell my sister she better have a good reason for skipping out on her own party. The rest of us have been here for hours working on this float."

Ryan's reply came back garbled. The building and its terrible service. "Say it again?" he asked.

"I said, would a girl be a good enough excuse?"

"What do you mean 'a girl'?" Nico straightened at Ryan's announcement. "Are you talking about a real girl, as in—?"

"A baby, yes." His brother-in-law gave a breathy laugh. "The most beautiful girl you'll ever see. Seven pounds, nine ounces and as perfect as her mother."

Nico's jaw dropped. He didn't know what to say. "Congratulations!" he finally managed to get out.

No sooner did he speak than Rafe nudged him with an elbow. "Baby?" he asked. Nico nodded, setting off a small cheer in the garage. Immediately, both Dani and Louisa dropped what they were doing to join Rafe by his side. "Boy or girl?" Louisa asked.

"A girl," he whispered back. It was hard to believe his baby sister was a mother herself. "How is Marianna?" he asked Ryan. "Is she all right?"

"She's fantastic. Amazing. When you see what a woman goes through to give birth…" Admiration laced every word Ryan said.

Nico felt a pang of jealousy in the face of such love and devotion. His eyes sought Louisa, who waited for details with folded hands pressed to her lips and eyes turned sapphire with anticipation. Like everyone else, her emotions showed on her face. Everyone but him, that was. His insides were numb as he struggled to process Ryan's news.

The gulf that separated him from others in the world widened. *See?* He wanted to tell Rafe. *People don't always change.*

He certainly hadn't.

CHAPTER NINE

MARIANNA WORE MOTHERHOOD as though it was a designer dress. Sitting on the living room sofa of her villa, wearing pajamas and a terry cloth robe, she'd never looked lovelier. Every time she looked down at the bundle sleeping in the bassinet, her face glowed with contentment. "We named her Rosabella," she said to Louisa, who was sitting next to her. "Rosa for short."

"She's beautiful," Louisa said. As peaceful as an angel, her little lips parted in slumber. It was all Louisa could do not to run her finger along a downy cheek.

"The nurses said not to be fooled by how much she's sleeping," she said. "In a day or two she'll be wanting to nurse all the time."

"Then we'll be wishing she'd sleep," Ryan added. He looked as smitten as his wife.

"What do you mean, *we*? I'm going to be the one doing all the work. You'll probably just roll over and go back to sleep."

"Ah, *amore mio*, you know I'd help nurse if I could. It would let me bond with the baby."

"Then it's a good thing I bought you this," Louisa said, reaching for the pastel pink gift bag she'd set on the floor. She'd almost said "we." Living and working with Nico the past week had her thinking of them as a pair.

"A breast pump!" Marianna announced with what could almost be described as evil glee. "Thank you, Louisa; it's perfect. Looks like you'll be able to bond with the baby after all, *amore mio*."

"Yes, Louisa," Ryan said, much less enthusiastically. "It's exactly what we needed."

They were both exaggerating for effect. From the moment he'd learned of the pregnancy, Ryan had been determined to be as active a father as possible. Louisa had no doubt he would be awake every time no matter who did the actual feeding. She looked over at Nico, to see what he was thinking. The man had barely said a word since their arrival. In fact, he'd been unusually quiet since Ryan had called to announce little Rosa's arrival. Currently, he stood next to the bassinet, staring down at the sleeping baby.

"She's so tiny," he said.

"Not for long," Marianna replied. "She's got her father's appetite. Would you like to hold her, Uncle Nico?"

At his sister's suggestion, Nico paled. "I wouldn't want to wake her…"

"You won't, and if she does wake up, she'll probably fall right back to sleep. The little angel has had a busy couple of days. Haven't you, Rosa?" Adoration beaming from every feature of his face, Ryan ran the back of his finger along his daughter's cheek. "You might as well get used to being hands-on," he said to Nico. "No way is your sister going to let you get out of babysitting."

"Absolutely. With Angelo living in the States and Ryan's family in Australia, you're the only family she has in Monte Calanetti. Now hold her. I want a photo for her baby album."

"Better do what your sister says," Ryan said.

The vintner's face was the picture of anxiety as Ryan placed the swaddled baby in Nico's arms. Looking as if he'd rather be doing anything else, he balanced Rosa's head in the palm of one hand while the other held her bottom.

"She's not a bottle of wine," Marianna admonished. "Hold her close. And smile. I don't want her first memory of her uncle to be that he's a grouch."

"Forgive me; I've never held a baby before," Nico replied. But he did what he was told.

It made for a beautiful photo. Nico with his bronzed movie-star features, baby Rosa with her pink newborn skin. Something was off, though. Louisa couldn't say exactly what, but something about Nico's eyes didn't fit. For one thing, they lacked the sparkle she'd come to associate with his smiles. They looked darker—sad, even—and distant. Not unlike the way they'd looked the other day when Marianna visited.

Did his sister notice? Probably not, since the new mother was too busy directing the photo session. "Go stand next to Nico," she ordered. "We need one of the three of you."

"Um… You want me in your baby album?" Louisa wasn't sure that was a good idea.

"Of course. Why wouldn't I?" Marianna waved at her to move. "Go."

"Sooner you do it, the sooner she'll be done taking photos," Nico said.

She took her place by Nico's shoulder, and wondered if she would ever get used to being welcome. It didn't dawn on her until after Marianna showed her the pictures on her phone that she was in her most casual clothes and not wearing a stitch of makeup. The woman smiling back at her from the view screen looked like someone she used to know a long time ago, before she ever heard the name Steven Clark. Someone she hadn't seen in a long time. Maybe she'd stick around a little while.

"You make an attractive family," Marianna teased. "Maybe I should sell it to the papers."

"You do, and I'll return my breast pump." That she could have such an exchange without blanching spoke volumes about how well she was recovering from the scandal. She turned her attention back to the phone screen, her gaze moving from her face to Nico's to Rosa's and back to Nico's. There was definitely distance in Nico's smile...

Meanwhile, Ryan had retrieved Rosa, who hadn't woken up, and was tucking her into her bassinet. "I meant to tell you," he said, "the cradle fits the space perfectly."

"I'm glad," Nico replied.

"Nico had the family cradle restored," Marianna explained.

"He did?" She hadn't known, although knowing his respect for tradition, the gesture didn't surprise her.

"It has been in our family for generations," he replied, eyes still on the baby. "Made sense that it be used by the first member of the next generation."

"The piece is almost too beautiful for Rosa to sleep in," Ryan said.

"Come with me; I'll show you."

After casting a protective glance into the bassinet Marianna led her toward the nursery. "You know, I almost took the baby monitor with me," she said as they walked up the stairs. "But I thought that might be overprotective."

"With Ryan sitting five feet away from her, I would say yes," Louisa teased. Her friend's extreme mothering was adorable. Might not be so cute when

Rosa was older, but seeing as how Marianna had only been a mother for two days, she couldn't help smiling. The Amatuccis didn't do things halfway, did they?

The room was a baby's paradise. The couple had forgone traditional baby colors in favor of restful lavender, browns and greens. The Tuscan hillside, Louisa realized. Stuffed animals and books already filled the shelves, and there were, not one, but two mobiles, one hanging over what looked to be a small play area in the corner.

On the back wall hung a large landscape of the vineyards with baby animals playing peek-a-boo among the vines. Louisa spied a rabbit and a kitten straight off. "Logan Cascini's wife, Lucia, painted it as a baby gift," Marianna told her. "There are supposed to be eleven different baby animals hiding in the fields. So far Ryan and I can only find eight."

"It's amazing." This was a gift that would amuse a child for years to come. Something Louisa would want for her own child. "Makes my breast pump look lame," she said.

As exquisite as the painting was, however, it paled in comparison to the cradle below it. Ryan hadn't exaggerated. It was gorgeous. It wasn't that the piece was fancy; in fact the design was actually very modest, but you could feel its history. The tiny nicks and dents told the story of all the Amatuccis that had slept safe in its confines. She ran her hand along the sideboard. The restorer had done a great job, polishing the olive wood to a gleaming dark brown without destroying what made it special.

"My great-grandfather built this when my grand-father was born. According to my father, it was because my great-grandmother demanded he not sleep in a drawer. Baby Amatuccis have slept in it ever since."

Louisa tried to picture Nico as a baby with his thick dark curls. Bet he had a smile that could melt your heart.

She wondered why he hadn't told her what he was planning. But then, why would he? No doubt the idea came to him when Marianna had announced her pregnancy. If she recalled, the two of them had hardly been friends at the time. Not like they were now.

Actually she wasn't sure what they were to each other anymore. Did a friend lie in bed listening for the sound of footsteps in the hall, relieved yet disap-pointed when the steps didn't draw near her door? Did a friend watch her friend while he worked, wondering what it might feel like to run her hands down his muscular arms? Louisa doubted it. Yet she had done both those things the past couple of days.

Then there was the fact she was continuing to stay at the vineyard. The headlines had stopped. There was little reason she shouldn't return to the palazzo and start figuring out what she wanted to do for the future.

So how come the two of them were continuing to cohabitate as though they were a couple?

"...godparents."

She realized Marianna was talking. "I'm sorry," she said. "I was thinking about something else."

"Here I thought I was the one with distractions," the brunette teased. "Please tell me you'll pay better attention to your goddaughter."

"G-goddaughter?" Was Marianna asking what Louisa thought she was asking?

"Ryan and I were hoping you would be Rosabella's godmother."

Godmother? She had to have misunderstood. In Italy, a godparent was expected to play a huge role in a child's life. More like a second parent. And they were asking *her*?

That's why they'd insisted on including her in the photograph. "Are—are you sure?" she asked. "There isn't someone you want more?" Her brother Angelo's wife, for example.

"Ryan and I can't think of anyone we'd want more," the brunette said, reaching over and resting a hand atop hers.

"But the scandal?"

"Who cares about the scandal? The scandal is what makes you so perfect. We want our daughter to grow up knowing that doing the right thing isn't always easy, but that truly strong people find a way to make it through."

Louisa couldn't breathe for the lump in her throat. Marianna and Ryan...they thought her brave? Talk about ironic. She'd felt nothing but fear from the day she discovered Steven's duplicity. "All I did was tell the authorities the truth." And seize an opportunity to escape.

"You did more than tell the truth. You paid a price publicly. It couldn't have been easy being destroyed by the press the way you were. That's the kind of person I want to help guide my daughter. A woman who's strong enough to bounce back."

Had she really, though? Bounced back? There were still so many fears holding her back. She wasn't sure she'd ever completely escape Steven.

Still, the invitation meant more than Marianna would ever realize. Louisa felt the tears pushing at her eyes. Seemed like all she did was tear up lately. "You just want me to give you a better baby gift," she said, sniffing them away.

Marianna's eyes were watery. "So is that a yes?"

"Yes!" Louisa didn't stop to think twice. "I would be honored."

"Perfect. I'm so happy." The brunette clapped her hands together the way a child might when getting a special gift. "This will be perfect. You can teach Rosa how to be strong and gracious, and her godfather will teach her how to be smart and respect tradition. Along with winemaking, that is."

Wine? "Who are you going to ask to be god-father?" she asked. As if she didn't know. There was only one man who fit that description.

Her friend looked at her with surprise. "Nico, of course."

Of course.

"Is that a problem?"

Only in the sense that she and Nico would be bound together for the rest of Rosa's life. Flutters took over her insides.

"No, no problem," she said.

Marianna's reply was preempted by a high-pitched wail coming from downstairs.

"Looks like I didn't need to bring the monitor after all," the new mother said. "Rosa has inherited my lungs."

"Ryan and Marianna are going to have their hands full fending off the boys when Rosa's older, that's for sure," Louisa said as they crossed the plaza a short while later. "I won't be surprised if Ryan decides to ship her off to a convent when she's older just to keep them away."

"Yes," Nico replied. "Because naturally Italy is full of convents where the residents can hide their children."

"It's an expression, Nico."

"I know what it is." He tightened his grip on the shopping bag he was carrying, the plastic handle threatening to snap in two from the pressure. The knot at the base of his neck had been tightening since they'd left Marianna's villa, fed by his companion's continual gushing over baby Rosabella. How beautiful, how sweet, how tiny, how wonderful. Every adjective reminding him of his shortcomings, because he felt *nothing*.

"I'm sure Ryan will deal with the onslaught of suitors when the time comes," he told her.

"I'm sure he will, too." She looked at him with a frown. "What gives? You've been in a bad mood all morning. Is everything all right?"

No. Everything was horrible. How else could it be when the world decided to remind you of unvarnished truths? "I have a lot to do at the winery, is all."

"You sure that's all it is?"

"What else would it be?" he asked, in a casual voice. Thank goodness for his sunglasses. He wasn't sure his eyes looked nearly as impassive as his voice sounded.

"I don't know. I was wondering if it had something to do with baby Rosa."

He stumbled over a cobblestone. "Contrary to what you think, the birth of baby Rosa is not the biggest event taking place in this town."

"No, but it is the biggest thing to happen to your

family. I would think you'd be happy for Marianna and Ryan."

"I am happy for them." Granted he hadn't been thrilled when he'd first discovered Marianna was pregnant by a man she barely knew, but since then Ryan had proven himself devoted to both his sister and their child. "I hope Rosa is the first of many children."

"Good, because back at the villa you looked like you didn't want anything to do with the baby."

On the contrary. He turned to look at her. "I wanted plenty."

If Louisa caught the pointedness in his comment, she let it pass. They'd reached the town center. It being only a few days until the festival, tourists crowded the cobblestone square. Camera phones at the ready, they posed in front of the fountain and raised them to snap pictures of brightly decorated balconies. Many carried shopping bags like his. Monte Calanetti's economy was still going strong. Rafe would be happy. A lot of these people were no doubt eating at Mancini's this evening.

As though by mutual agreement, he and Louisa stopped in the square where they'd had their first kiss. He wondered how often she thought of that afternoon. As often as he did? Thinking of their kiss had become practically an obsession.

He wasn't sure if nature was trying to soothe him by pointing out that he could at least feel physical passion, or if she were mocking him by giving him a pointless attraction.

To rub salt into his wounds, he stole a long look at Louisa's profile. The way her hair turned white in the bright sun was something he'd never grow tired of studying. He loved the way her hair wasn't one color but a collection of platinum and gold strands woven together to create a shade that was uniquely Louisa. It was her hair, no doubt, that had caught Steven Clark's attention on the elevator. Had his fingers itched to comb through the colors the way Nico's did?

Louisa turned in his direction, and he quickly looked away.

"Did your sister tell you she asked me to be Rosabella's godmother?" she asked him.

"She did?" He hadn't known, but he wasn't surprised. Marianna had told him how much she'd come to care about Louisa these past months.

"She said she picked me because I could teach her daughter about being strong. Funny, but I don't think of myself as strong."

Because she didn't give herself enough credit. "You're stronger than you think."

"Maybe," she said, looking away. The knot at the back of Nico's neck returned as he guessed what her next comment would be. "She told me they asked you to be the godfather."

"They did." For some insane reason, they actually wanted him as a backup parent. The question had caught him so off guard he couldn't answer.

"It's not going to be a problem, is it?" Louisa asked. "Being paired with me? I know it's a big deal here, and if you'd rather stand up with someone else..."

"What? No." He hadn't stopped to think that his unenthusiastic answer might sound like an objection to her. "I think you'll be a wonderful godmother. It's me that I'm worried about."

"If you're afraid you're going to drop her..."

"No, I'm not afraid of dropping her."

"Then, what's the matter?"

"It's complicated," he replied. Hoping she'd drop the subject, Nico walked toward the fountain.

Monte Calanetti's famed nymph reclined across her rocks, the clamshell in her hand beckoning to all who wanted to toss a coin. Based on the silver and gold coins shimmering beneath the water, a lot of tourists had tried today. "Have you ever wished on the fountain?" he asked when he felt Louisa standing behind him. A silly question. Everyone in Monte Calanetti had tried at least once to land a coin in the clamshell.

"Sure," she replied. "My coin missed the shell, though."

"Mine always missed, too."

"And I thought you were perfect."

She was joking, but Nico grimaced all the same. He was most definitely not perfect.

So much for changing the subject. "Didn't matter. My wish came true anyway," he replied.

"What did you used to wish for?"

"That I wouldn't be like my parents. In and out of love. Jumping from one drama to another. I would not live on an emotional roller coaster."

Her hand came to rest between his shoulder blades, the warmth from the contact reaching through his linen shirt. "Can't blame you there," she said "Who would?"

No one, or so he'd thought, which was why he'd stood here as a little boy and tossed coin after coin. He could see himself, standing at the fountain's edge, his jaw clenched with determination. "Unfortunately, it worked too well," he said, with a sigh.

"You're confusing me."

Of course he was. Louisa felt things deeply. He saw the warmth in her eyes when she looked at Rosa, the immediate affection. His sister couldn't have picked a better woman to help guide his niece through life. She would love Baby Rosa like her own. Unlike…

Fear gripped his chest. "Everyone sees me as some kind of leader," he said. "A man they can count on."

"Because you are. You certainly hold Monte

Calanetti together. Not to mention the vineyard, the palazzo."

"Those are things, businesses. Anyone can manage a business. People, on the other hand…" He took off his sunglasses, wanting her to see how serious he was regarding his question. "What if I let her down?"

"Who?"

"Baby Rosa. What if she can't count on me? What if I can't love her enough to be there emotionally when she needs me to?"

"You're serious? That's why you kept pulling away when we talked about the baby." She sank to sit on the fountain wall. "Do you really believe you won't be able to care about your own niece?"

"Care about, yes, but care enough?" He shook his head. "I've already proven I can't."

"When? Oh, your fiancée."

"My fiancée." Taking a space next to her, he let his shopping bag rest on the ground between his feet. Thankfully the noontime heat had chased many of the tourists to the shade, leaving them momentarily alone.

"Floriana was a wonderful girl. Smart, beautiful, kind. We shared all the same interests. We never ever argued."

"She sounds perfect."

"She was," he said, staring at his hands. "We were perfect for each other." The answer tasted sour on his tongue. In a way, singing Floriana's praises to Louisa felt wrong.

"What happened?"

"Simple," he said. "I broke her heart."

There had to be more to the story. Something that Nico wasn't telling her. The man she knew wouldn't carelessly break a woman's heart.

Although wasn't that exactly the kind of man she'd thought he was when she'd met him?

Yes, she had, but she knew better now. Knew him better now. "Surely it's not as simple as that," she said.

"Ah, but it is," he replied. "As perfect as Floriana was—as we were for each other—I couldn't love her. Not truly and deeply, the way a person should be loved. That's when I realized I'll never be like my parents or like Angelo or Marianna. I don't have it in me."

"It?"

"Passion. Real, deep emotion.

"It's true," he said when Louisa opened her mouth to argue. "Angelo and Marianna, they are like my parents. They feel things. Highs. Lows. Excitement. They thrive on it, even. But me… I don't want highs and lows. I want calm. I want…"

"Consistency," Louisa supplied. Certainty. To know when he walked through the door that his world hadn't been turned upside down. She had the sudden flash that Nico had been as trapped by his parents' chaos as she had been by Steven's control.

"Consistency is one way of putting it, I suppose. Much better than saying I lack depth."

"Is that what Floriana said? She was wrong."

"Was she?"

"Just because you don't throw plates like your parents doesn't mean you're not capable of passion." It killed her to hear him beat himself up so needlessly. Couldn't he see how impossibly wrong he was about himself? She'd witnessed his passion plenty of times. In the vineyards when he talked about Carlos. When he talked of Monte Calanetti's traditions.

When he'd kissed her. She'd never felt such passion before.

Nico stared at his hands as if they held the argument he needed. "Then why didn't I feel anything today?" he asked. "The three of you—Marianna, Ryan, you—you couldn't stop oohing and aahing at Baby Rosa. Meanwhile, the only thing going through my mind was that she looked...small."

"What did you expect to think? She's three days old. It's not like she's going to be filled with personality."

"But everyone else..."

Okay, now she wanted to shake him and make him see sense. For a smart man, he was being incredibly stupid. "Marianna and Ryan are her parents. If she wrinkles her nose they think it's a sign of genius."

"And you…"

"I'm a woman. I'm programmed to think babies are adorable. You, on the other hand, are a guy. Until babies actually do something, you don't see the point.

"Look," she said. Grasping his face between her hands, she forced him to look her in the eye to make sure he heard what she was saying. "Just because a person seems perfect doesn't mean they are. Believe me, I know. You're going to make a wonderful godfather. The very fact you're worrying about doing a good job shows how much you care.

"Besides," she added, "I refuse to do this godmother thing without a good partner. Last time I looked, we made a pretty good team."

The worry faded from around his eyes. Giving her a grateful smile, Nico rested his forehead against hers. His hands came up to cup her face. "Thank you, *bella mia*," he said, the whisper caressing her lips. Louisa closed her eyes and let the sensation wash over her.

They sat entwined like that for several minutes, neither in a rush to break the moment. As far as she was concerned, she could sit there all afternoon. She didn't even care if there were paparazzi watching.

CHAPTER TEN

THE NEXT DAY, a cold front invaded the valley and everyone feared the harvest festival would be threatened by rain. "The tourists will still come," Nico had said as they gathered to finish the float. "We've never failed to attract a crowd, rain or shine."

"But sun brings a better crowd," Marianna had been quick to point out, "and this is the one year when we can count on the crowd being especially large."

Turned out Nico's sister needn't have worried. The morning of the festival, Louisa woke to see the sun brightening a cloudless blue sky.

"Luck is on our side," Nico had remarked over coffee before adding, "Perfect day for playing festival queen."

"Nice try," she'd answered, "but no." With the headlines diminishing daily, why court trouble?

Nevertheless, she agreed to accompany him to the parade's staging ground to give their float a proper send-off. While he was in the shower, she snuck over to the palazzo and got out a tiered skirt and peasant blouse from her closet. A peace offering. She might not be queen, but she could dress in the spirit of the occasion.

The thought didn't occur to her until she was ducking through the archway leading to Nico's villa, that if she was comfortable enough crossing the fields alone, she could move back home.

Tomorrow.

For so many years her thoughts had revolved around escaping—escaping Steven, escaping Boston, escaping the paparazzi—and suddenly here she was focused on staying.

Something had shifted between her and Nico that day at the fountain. There was a depth to their friendship she hadn't felt before. An openness brought about by shared fears. Whereas before there had been attraction, she felt pulled by an attraction of a different sort. Didn't make sense, she knew. But there it was.

"Wow," Nico said when stepped back into the kitchen. "Like a proper Tuscan peasant."

Appreciation lit his eyes, turning her insides warm. She hadn't done all that much. "Thank you. I figured when in Rome, or in this case Tuscany..."

"You look just like a proper Tuscan gypsy." And he, a proper Tuscan vintner in his jeans and loose white shirt. Louisa had never seen him look more appealing. He offered his hand. "Shall we?"

The festival itself was to be held in the plaza. Last night Nico and several of his employees had gone into town to set up a quintet of large half barrels around the fountain, and so she assumed that was where they were heading for the parade, as well. To her surprise, however, he turned his truck toward Comparino. "We start at the palazzo," he told her, "and head into town, recreating the route the farmers took back when the *mezzadria* system was in place. That's when the sharecroppers would present the landowners with their share of the harvest. Back then the Bertonellis would have used the grapes to make wine. Today we use a lesser quality crop and put the fruit in the vats for stomping."

"I can't believe people still stomp grapes." Louisa thought the tradition was reserved only for movies and old sitcoms.

"Tourists come from all over the world to see Old World traditions. The least we can do is provide them."

She bet Nico loved every minute of them, too, lover of tradition that he was. In fact, there was a special kind of glow about him this morning. He looked brighter, more alive. His body hummed with energy, too, more so than usual. Standing by his side, she found it impossible not to let it wash over her, as well.

They turned a corner and drove into a field that

had become a makeshift parade ground. In addition to the floats, Louisa spied dozens of townspeople dressed in costume. There were women wearing woolen folk dresses and large straw hats and men dressed as peasant farmers. She spotted musicians and what she guessed were dancers, as well.

"Later on, they'll demonstrate the *trescone*," Nico said. "Everyone present is invited to join in."

And here she thought the festival was just an excuse to eat and drink.

"Can I ask you a question?" she asked once Nico had parked the truck. "Why is tradition so important to you?" She suspected she already knew the answer, but wanted to hear it from him.

"I don't know," he replied. "I suppose it is because tradition helps define who we are and what we do. There's a sacred quality to knowing that you're walking in the footsteps of generations that came before you. Time has passed, but the traditions, the core of who we are, doesn't change."

In other words, he loved the consistency. For a man whose entire life had been fraught with chaos, tradition—like Carlos's vineyard—never let him down. No wonder he'd been so adamant that she lead the parade.

And yet, he was willing to let go of tradition to make her feel more comfortable. Once again, he was rushing to her rescue.

Maybe it was time she returned the favor. "I'll do it," she said.

"Do what?"

"I'll lead the parade."

If everything else went wrong today, the way Nico's eyes lit up would be reason enough for her answer. "Are you sure?" he asked her.

"Absolutely." What were a few miles, right? She could do it. "But only if you'll walk with me."

"Are you asking if I'll be your king?"

Dear Lord, the way he said the sentence… Her insides grew warm. "Don't be literal," she said, trying to hide her reaction by making light of the comment. "More like a royal companion who's there to help me when I screw up."

Damn if the way he brushed a tendril of hair off her cheek before speaking didn't turn her inside out. "It would be my pleasure, *bella mia*."

Royal companion wasn't the right term at all. Nico was a king. Smiling brightly and waving to the crowds, he belonged at the front of the parade far more than Louisa did. The town loved him.

Or maybe Monte Calanetti was just full of love today. The streets were lined with revelers who laughed and cheered them along as they wound their way slowly down the cobblestone streets. Behind them, the costumed men carried baskets of grapes while the women tossed bags of sugared nuts they had stored in the pockets of their aprons. If photographers were there, they were hidden by the throngs of tourists who, it was clear, were only interested in enjoying the day.

"Signorina! Signorina!" A little girl wearing a dress the colors of Italy, ran into the street carrying a crown made from ribbons and roses. *"Per voi la Signorina Harrison,"* she said, holding it in her hands. *"Una corona per la regina."*

Louisa beamed her. A crown? For her? *"Grazie,"* she said, placing the flowers on her head. The wreath was too big and slid down to her ears, but Louisa didn't care. She grinned and flicked the ribbons over her shoulder.

There were more children. More flowers presented. Too many for Louisa to carry, so she began giving them to the women behind her, running from the front of the parade to the rear and back again. It became a game between her and the children, to see how fast she could run the gamut before another flower appeared. By the time they reached the fountain, she was laughing and gasping for breath.

"Told you the town wouldn't care," Nico whispered in her ear. She turned to discover his eyes glittered with laughter, too. "This is amazing," she told him.

"You are having fun, then?"

Was he joking? What she was feeling at this moment was so much more than amusement. She felt free. All those years of being the outsider were but bad memories. She'd found a place where she'd belonged. A home.

To think, if Nico hadn't gone to the palazzo the day the headlines broke—if he hadn't insisted she stay—she might still be looking.

What would she have done without him?

"I'm having a wonderful time," she said. She moved to throw her arms around him in a hug only to be thwarted by the enveloping crowd. Having emptied their baskets into three oversize half barrels, the marchers stood clapping rhythmically. "They're waiting for you," Nico told her. "The queen is the first to stomp the grapes."

As though they'd been waiting, two of the men wearing medieval costumes appeared at her elbows and began guiding her forward. "Wait, wait," she said, laughing. "I still have my shoes on."

"Just kick them off," a familiar voice hollered. Looking left, she saw Dani waving from a few feet away. "I'll grab them for you," her friend said.

She made her way to the front barrel that, despite its size, was overflowing with large bunches of purple grapes.

"I'm not doing this without my royal companion," she said, looking over her shoulder.

Evidently the crowd thought this a wonderful idea, because a second later, Nico was pushed into the circle. As he stepped closer, his laugh faded to a mischievous gleam. "Now you've asked for it, *bella mia*."

Grabbing her by the waist, he lifted her in the air and plopped her feetfirst into the barrel.

Louisa shrieked as the grapes squished between her toes. "It's cold!"

"You expected a warm bath?" he asked with a laugh. Stepping into the barrel with her, he took her by the hands. "Be careful, it's slippery."

No kidding. The crushed grapes and skin quickly stuck to the bottom of the container, creating a layer of slickness. Twice already, she would have lost her balance if Nico hadn't been holding her up. Still, as cold and slippery as the grapes were, it was fun marching in place. Particularly with Nico's hands sending warmth up her arms.

A few minutes later, the rest of the crowd joined them, kicking off their shoes and crowding into the vats. Laughter abounded as everyone was eager to take their turn mashing the grapes to a pulp.

"I can't believe this is how people used to make wine," she said to him over the noise. "They must have had incredibly muscular thighs."

"Not really." Nico had leaned in to speak. His breath floated over her collarbone leaving goose bumps. "Italian winemakers have used presses to crush grapes since the middle ages. This is just for the tourists."

"You mean there is no Old World tradition?"

"Not that I know of."

"I'm up to my ankles in pulverized grapes because of a gimmick? You—"

He laughed and she gave his shoulder a shove, only to have her feet slide out from beneath her.

"Careful!" Nico scooped her up into his arms just as she was about to fall bottom first into the mashed fruit. "We wouldn't want you to be trampled," he said, smiling down at her.

No danger of that now. With her arms wrapped around his neck, and his arms holding her tight, Louisa had never felt safer. "I'm not worried," she said. "You'd rescue me."

His smile faded. "Always."

Louisa's breath caught at the seriousness in his voice. Just as it had at the royal wedding, the world receded, leaving only the two of them and the sound of their breathing. Nico's eyes grew heavy lidded, his attention focused on Louisa's mouth. Slowly she ran a tongue over her lower lip, an action for which she was rewarded with the tightening of his hand on her waist. "Louisa…" His voice was rough and raw.

He wanted her. But he was holding back to let her make the first move. That she held the power was all Louisa needed to reach a decision.

She pulled his head down to meet hers…

Dear Lord, how on earth could she have gone so

long without kissing him? Nico might have given her the power to decide, but once their mouths joined, he took control, kissing her so deeply Louisa couldn't tell where she ended and he began. She didn't care. She was too swept away by the moment.

It was the cheer rising from the crowd that finally broke the moment. "I think the crowd approves," Nico said, rubbing his nose against hers.

Heat rushed to Louisa's cheeks. Let the crowd cheer, she decided. She held his gaze and wondered if her eyes looked as blown and glazed over as his.

"Why don't we go someplace more private?" he said. Without giving her a chance to answer, he carried her out of the barrel and through the crowd.

Nico pressed a kiss to the head resting on his shoulder. Louisa and he were in his garden, ensconced on a lounger beneath the pergola. Insects could be heard buzzing in the foliage above, their soft droning working with the wine to make him comfortable and drowsy. An interesting sensation, since only an hour before he'd been consumed with lust. Once alone, the urgency had receded. The best wines were made with patience. So it was with lovemaking, as well. They had all night. Why rush when you could draw out the pleasure?

Besides, strange as it seemed, being close to Louisa like this was pleasure itself.

"What was she like?"

Her question came out of nowhere. "Who?" he asked, fingers playing with the tendrils of her hair.

"Your fiancée."

"Floriana? Why do you ask? Are you jealous?" That she might be gave him a jolt of satisfaction.

"I'm curious. What made her so perfect?"

He thought back. "I told you, she liked the same things I liked, she had the same sense of humor. Plus we wanted the same things out of life."

"Which were?"

"To create wine and live a life free of drama."

"I take it you never threw a reporter off her balcony."

"She didn't own a balcony,"

"You know what I mean."

"Yes, I do." Floriana would never need to take refuge in his winery to avoid scandal. Rational to a fault, she would never have fallen for a man like Steven in the first place. On the other hand, she also never ignited a fire in the pit of his stomach the way Louisa did. Standing in those grapes, with that silly floral crown falling about her ears and her clothes wrinkled and damp from the heat, Louisa had been the most gorgeous thing he'd ever seen.

"She sounds like someone Steven would have liked. Whenever I found an interest Steven didn't like, he would find a way to suck the fun out of it."

"I don't understand." The American colloquialism threw him, although he could wager a guess.

"Well…" She shifted so she could prop herself up on one elbow. "He would either get condescending and make me feel like it was silly, or he'd suggest it wasn't the kind of thing 'Mrs. Steven Clark' should be doing."

The man was a bully. Nico was glad they'd put him in prison. Her ex deserved to be locked up in a cell as lonely and sad as he'd made his wife.

"He didn't deserve you. You know that."

"When we met, I thought I didn't deserve him."

A most foolish notion. If anything Steven Clark must have known from the start that he'd discovered a treasure and that was why he'd insisted on wrapping her up so tightly.

"What's sad is how I was so impressed by something that wasn't real. I mean, all his power and breeding. Turned out he wasn't any better than me."

"You were the better one," Nico said. "To begin with, you weren't a thief."

Louisa smiled. "Thanks, but I meant background-wise. He was just some guy from the Midwest. His fancy family history was as phony as his investment scheme. When I contacted the feds, the whole house of cards came tumbling down. The only truly real thing that survived was the palazzo." She nestled back against the curve of his neck, her hand coming up to play with the edge of his shirt collar.

"Thank God, I never told him about the place or it would be gone, too."

Prison was too good for him. "The bastard is lucky he wasn't the one on your balcony," he muttered.

"Might have been interesting if he was. I think I'd have liked to see you throw him over."

"Satisfying, too," Nico said. Propping himself on an elbow, he smiled down at her face. "What is it about you that incites me to violence?"

"I don't know."

Neither did he, and he'd been looking for the answer for the past few weeks. All he knew was that the idea of Louisa hurting made him see red. He wanted to punish Steven and the others for making her life so hard.

Come to think of it, Louisa made him feel a lot of strong emotions. He didn't just want to kiss her, he wanted to kiss her senseless. And he didn't want to enjoy her company, he wanted to spend every moment he could spare with her.

Where on earth did these feelings come from? He'd never behaved this way around Floriana. Or anyone else for that matter.

Could it be that this—Louisa—was what he'd been missing all these years?

He turned on his side until they lay face-to-face. All it took was one look into her blue eyes and his pulse started racing again. "Thank you," she whispered.

"You don't have to thank me for anything."

"But I do. Did you know," she asked as he freed a stray petal from her hair, "that this past week was the first time in years that I've felt like I truly belonged."

"I'm not surprised. Monte Calanetti loves you."

"No, Monte Calanetti loves you. I'm just lucky to have won approval from its favorite son."

"Oh, you have more than my approval, *bella mia*." She'd awakened a part of him he didn't think existed and now it belonged to her forever.

Suddenly, his desire couldn't wait any longer. Slanting his mouth across hers, he drank in her sweet taste. This—this—was perfection, he realized. All these years he believed his soul was incomplete, it had merely been in hibernation, waiting for his blonde American to move in next door.

"Louisa, Louisa, Louisa," he chanted, his lips raining kisses down her throat. "I've waited for so long."

He paused when he reached the lace neckline blocking the rest of her skin from exploration. The top button strained to be released. All it would take was a flick of his fingers.

His hand hovered. The memory of her pushing him away at the royal wedding forced him to slow down. "Are you sure?"

Looking up, he saw eyes more black than blue, the pupils wide with desire. Out of the corner of his own eye, he saw a shaky hand reaching toward her blouse. She smiled, and a moment later, the button was undone.

It was all the answer Nico needed and he crushed his mouth to hers. Later, as his fingers made short work of the remaining buttons and as Louisa breathed his name, he wondered if maybe it wasn't only Monte Calanetti that was in love…

"You are a lying lie-face. I hope you know that."

What the heck? Louisa blinked at the nightstand clock and decided it was far too early to decipher what Dani meant.

"I just want you to know that I forgive you," her friend continued.

"Forgive me for what?" She brushed the hair from her eyes.

"For telling me nothing was going on between you and Nico, of course. You're not going to keep insisting the two of you are only friends after what we saw yesterday."

Louisa smiled, thinking about what Dani and the others hadn't seen. "No."

"Good. Because unless you let all your friends literally sweep you off your feet, no one would believe you," Dani told her. "By the way, Rafe and I completely understand why the two of you wanted to keep things private for a while. Especially given the circumstances."

"Thank you." No sense explaining how she and Nico weren't together until yesterday. Like Dani said, after the way she'd kissed him in the plaza, no one would believe her anyway.

Nico had swept her off her feet, hadn't he? *In more ways than one.* Her stomach dropped a little at that.

He's not Steven. This was a different kind of affair.

"Louisa, are you there?"

She yawned and pushed herself to a sitting position. "I'm here," she said, pulling the sheet up.

"Good. I was afraid Nico might be distracting you."

"Nico isn't here. He went to see how the harvest was going." *I'll wake you when I get back*, he'd whispered upon kissing her cheek. So much for that fantasy. Maybe she could pretend to be asleep. "Is there a reason you're calling this early," she asked, "or did you just want to call me a liar?"

"I have your sandals. You left them in the plaza, in case you were looking for them." Oh, right. Now that she thought about it, Louisa didn't remember Nico getting his shoes either. Definitely wouldn't be able to sell the idea of friends.

"Thank you," she replied, sheepishly.

"Also now that the festival is over, Rafe wants our

economic development committee to start meeting in earnest. Can you ask Nico if he's available next Tuesday morning, since you'll probably see him before any of the rest of us will?"

Wow, the little blonde was really enjoying this wasn't she? Louisa shook her head, despite Dani's not being able to see her. "I'll try to track him down."

As if on cue, no sooner did she speak than the bedroom door opened and Nico strolled in wearing a shirt that should have been tossed several washes ago as it was at least a size too small. The fabric clung to his biceps and flat stomach.

When he saw her sitting up, he gave an exaggerated pout. "Dani," she mouthed. Her breath was too short to talk anyway. That shirt left nothing to the imagination, especially to a woman who knew exactly what lay beneath the cotton.

She watched him putter around the bedroom only half listening while Dani talked on about the meeting. Finally, guessing that a pause meant the conversation had ended, Louisa told Dani she had to go.

"What did Dani want?" Nico asked, when she tossed the phone aside.

"To give me grief for not telling her about our affair."

"But we weren't having an affair until…"

"I know," she replied. "And you didn't think people believed the tabloids."

"People will definitely believe them now," he

commented. Hard to call them liars, that was for sure. "Does it bother you?"

He looked so serious, standing there smoothing the wrinkled duvet. "Don't have much of a choice now, do I?" she replied. "I mean, the time to object would have been before I kissed you, and if I recall…"

She rolled onto her stomach, and hugged his pillow beneath her, grinning to herself at how the movement left her shoulders and back exposed. "As I recall, I wasn't doing all that much objecting at the time."

"That is true. I did not hear an objection," he replied. To her surprise, however, his smile didn't last. "I hope I don't hear one today."

An odd question considering she lay naked in his bed. "What could I possibly object to? That yesterday wasn't perfect enough?"

"This."

Louisa sat up as Nico pulled a rolled-up newspaper from the back of his waistband. The pages had been folded to a gossip column. Near the bottom of the page, she saw a brief mention of her holding court at the harvest festival with her latest millionaire boyfriend. Two lines. No more. Her fifteen minutes of notoriety was fading. A weight lifted from her shoulders.

"Looks like I've been replaced by bigger news."

Finally. Heaven help the poor person who took her place, whether they deserved the attention or not.

"So you don't mind the mention?" Nico asked.

Honestly? She'd rather they not mention her at all, but given how bad things had been? "Two lines on page thirteen I can handle."

At last, a true smile broke across Nico's face. "Good. I'm glad. I was concerned..."

"About what? That I would freak out?"

"You did before." He pressed a knee to the edge of the bed, and leaning close, cradled her face in his palm. "I never want anything to hurt you that badly again."

"*Never* is a very big promise," she told him.

"Not where you're concerned. If I have to buy up every newspaper in Italy to keep the paparazzi from hounding you, I will."

A shiver ran down Louisa's spine. *He's just trying to make you feel safe and special.* Even so, when he said things like that she couldn't help thinking of Steven.

"No need to do anything so drastic. I'll settle for your arms around me."

"Ask and you shall receive, *bella mia.*" A twinkle appeared in his eye. "Is a hug all you need?"

Well, when he looked at her like that... She grabbed the neck of his T-shirt and tugged him forward. "Now that you mention it, I might have a few other requests."

* * *

Following their lovemaking this morning, he'd wanted nothing more than to burrow with her beneath the sheets and, maybe after some rest, make love again. Unfortunately, Louisa insisted they needed to make an appearance at the winery before the gossip got too out of control.

As he leaned back against the bed watching her dress, he marveled at how light and full his chest felt. Never in his entire life could Nico remember feeling this way. It was as though overnight the entire world had grown brighter: every color more brilliant, every smell and sound more pronounced. And Louisa—beautiful, beautiful Louisa—he couldn't get enough of her. Not sexually, although making love with her was amazing, but of *her*. Her company, her presence, her happiness. It overwhelmed him how much he wanted to keep her close and protect her.

Suddenly, it hit him. He was in love.

For the first time in his life, he, Nico Amatucci, was truly, madly and deeply in love. The knowledge swelled inside him, inflating his heart until he thought it might burst.

To distract himself from the desire to haul her down the hall and back into his bed, he pretended to check the messages on his phone. Comprehension was difficult, what with his beautiful American standing a few feet away clad only in jeans and a bra.

"You should move your clothes into the closet," he said as he watched her taking a shirt from her suitcase. This long under his roof, and she hadn't unpacked? They would need to remedy that.

"Actually," Louisa said, "I was thinking it might be time for me to move back to the palazzo."

What? He sat a little straighter. "So soon?"

"It's hardly soon, Nico. I've been here two and a half weeks. This was only supposed to be until the press died down, remember?"

He remembered. He didn't want her to go. Her decision felt too much like her deciding to leave Monte Calanetti. How could she want to leave when they were only just were discovering their feelings.

It took all his effort to keep his voice light and not spoil the moment with his panic. "I suppose," he said, heaving the most dramatic sigh he could muster, "if you prefer to sleep alone in a cold palazzo than in my warm bed…"

"I never said I *preferred* the cold palazzo." She mocked his exaggerated voice with one of her own. "But I will have to go back eventually."

"I know. Not tonight, though?"

"Well…" He could tell from the sparkle in her eyes that she was only pretending to hesitate. "Okay, not tonight. But soon."

"Soon," he said, with a smile. He was surprised at how strongly he wanted her to stay. This new passionate self was going to take some getting used to.

Returning his attention to his phone, he noticed a message from Rafe. Agenda Items for Next Tuesday, the subject line read.

"Did Dani say any more about what Rafe wanted to talk about at this meeting?" he asked Louisa.

"Just that he wanted to get plans rolling on some type of event to attract visitors now that the harvest is wrapping up." She was buttoning the same silk blouse she'd worn when moving in. "He was thinking maybe something in February," she said. Around Valentine's Day."

"A holiday that will attract couples to his restaurant. Why am I not surprised?"

"Well, it is a romantic time of year. What could be more romantic than candlelit dinners with fine wine?"

"True." No sooner did she say the words than the image of the two of them nestled together in a corner table came to mind. "Very romantic indeed," he murmured.

"You could relabel one of your wines for the occasion. The winery must have something bubbly. A prosecco maybe?"

She was on to something. The winery had a very nice prosecco they produced on a limited basis. He could easily convince the local businesses to incorporate it into any plans they came up with.

Tossing his phone aside, he got up and, giving in partially to his desire, wrapped his arms around her waist. "Beautiful and brilliant," he said, kissing her neck. "You are definitely a prize worth keeping."

"Glad you think so."

Was it his imagination or did she tense slightly before breaking the embrace. She had a smile on her face, so he must have.

"Isn't Valentine's Day when you were hoping to open the palazzo to guests?" Since she obviously wasn't going to leave Monte Calanetti now, she could put her project back into motion.

To his surprise, she answered his question with a very sarcastic laugh. "I'm pretty sure those plans bit the dust when Dominic Merloni canceled our appointment."

Dominic Merloni. That shortsighted idiot. "He is not the only financier in Italy. There are other banks. Other sources of funding," he reminded her.

Louisa set down the hairbrush she was using to look at him. "Who's going to lend Luscious Louisa money? It was naive of me to think I could slide by on my maiden name. Too much of my past financial history is tied to Steven's."

"There is still the investor route. I'm sure there are plenty of people who would be interested. I've already said I would—"

"No." Her refusal was sharp and sudden, cutting him off. The reaction must have shown on his face, because her voice immediately softened. "We've already had this conversation Nico. I can't take money from you."

"Yes, but…" But that was before they became lovers. Surely, the situation had changed. Why not let him help?

"The whole idea of the hotel was to create something of my own," she said, cutting off his protest. "If I take money from you, then it won't feel that way. Especially now. The papers claim I'm dating you for your money," she added, picking up her brush.

"I thought you no longer cared what the papers said."

"I said I could deal with a small mention. What I don't want to do is give them more ammunition."

"So, what are you going to do? Give up on your plan?"

"I'm not 'giving up' on anything. The palazzo is going to make a wonderful hotel. Just not as soon as I hoped, is all. In another year or so, maybe, when I've had time to build a better financial profile."

Hearing Louisa put her dream on hold broke his heart. It wasn't right, her suffering another setback because of that cretin she'd married. Especially when he had the wealth and connections to make things happen.

Maybe… He looked down at his phone. Maybe

she wouldn't have to wait too long. Wouldn't hurt to make a few phone calls and see if he could open a few doors, would it?

CHAPTER ELEVEN

More than a few heads turned when Louisa and Nico entered the winery together. Dozens of pairs of eyes all staring knowingly in her direction.

Suppressing the old, familiar apprehension, Louisa nodded hello to everyone. "Looks like our secret is out," she said. The din of the machinery forced her to holler directly into Nico's ear.

He turned and looked at her with such concern, her heart wobbled. "Will you be all right?" he asked.

"I'll be fine." Even if she wouldn't, there was no way she could tell him that when he was looking at her so tenderly. "If I was worried about discretion, I wouldn't have kissed you in front of the whole village, would I?"

Nico looked about to reply when one of the workers called his name.

"Duty calls," he said. He flicked the hair from her eyes with his index finger. While not a kiss, the gesture was still intimate enough that, if there had been any employees who didn't suspect their affair, there weren't anymore.

Trying her best to look nonchalant, Louisa headed toward the back office. She was nodding hello to the women at the destemmer when she noticed the two men behind them exchanging euros.

"They've been placing bets ever since the picture of you and Signor Amatucci appeared in the paper," Mario said, appearing at her shoulder.

Bets. Her stomach churned a little at the news. "On what?"

"On you and Signor Amatucci. Half the staff believed the two of you were just friends; the other half was convinced the two of you had been together for months."

"Months? You must have heard wrong." Up until the royal wedding, she and Nico had only crossed paths when necessary, and half the time they'd butted heads.

The young man shrugged. "I only know what people told me."

"Which side were you on?" she asked.

"I don't like to place money on anyone who is writing me a reference."

"A smart man," she replied.

"For what it's worth," Mario continued, following her into the office "the majority were hoping the rumors turned out to be true."

"They were?" Come to think of it, while people

stared, nobody seemed particularly acrimonious. There were no cold shoulders like in Boston. In fact, Louisa realized, some of them had amusement in their eyes.

"Public consensus seems to be that it was high time Signor Amatucci had a serious relationship."

"It is, is it?"

"At least among the older female employees."

"I see." She wondered if Nico knew he had a mothering contingent. Probably.

Feeling slightly better, she sat down at her desk. Today's order list wasn't as long as previous days' as most people had purchased their bottles in person at the festival. She counted fewer than two dozen names.

"Those should be the last of the orders," Mario said. "We'll be out of Amatucci Reserve after today."

"Guess that means my job will be finishing soon, as well. No wine, no need to fulfill orders." With the headlines dying down and the wine gone, it was definitely time to go home.

"That's too bad," Mario replied. "You'll be missed."

"I know. What will people have to bet on?"

"I'm serious. I'll admit, when you first arrived some of us were concerned. We didn't know what to expect. But then we got to know you, and we realized what Signor Amatucci said at the staff meeting was true…"

"I'm sorry." Louisa put down the paper she'd picked up. "What staff meeting?"

"Right after you started. *Signor* held a staff meeting and told us the headlines were all exaggerations and that we should make a point of getting to know you."

So that's why Mario and the others had warmed up to her. Because Nico had told them to. "How very kind of him," she replied. Inside, she wanted to wring Nico's neck.

"Well, like *signor* said, once we got to know you, we'd realize we shouldn't believe everything we read. At least I don't believe it."

"Thank you." She did her best to keep her voice calm and kind. The young man was being sincere. Besides, her annoyance wasn't with him, it was with his boss.

"This reminds me…" Palms pressed to the desk top, she pushed herself to her feet, deliberately moving slowly so as to stay calm. "There's something I wanted to ask Nico about today's orders. Do you mind?"

"Not at all. I saw him and Vitale heading toward the wine cellar."

Perfect. They could talk without being overheard.

Cool and dark, the wine cellar Nico had proudly told her about on her first day had changed little from when the Amatuccis first started making wine. The stone walls and floor were the same ones against which his great-grandfather had stacked his wine barrels. At the moment the tradition meant little as she stalked the floor-to-ceiling stacks looking for Nico.

She found him in the farthest room, clipboard in hand. Soon as he saw her, a smile broke across his face. "Now here is a pleasant coincidence. I was just imagining what it would be like to bring you down here and have my way with you."

"You'll have to keep imagining," she replied, sidestepping his grasp.

Immediately his smile turned into a frown. "Is something wrong?"

"You tell me. Did you really tell your employees they had to be nice to me?"

"Where did you hear that?"

"Mario told me about your staff meeting." Not that it mattered who'd told her. The way he was avoiding looking her in the eyes told her it was true.

The irritation she'd been tamping down, quickly roared to life, making it a herculean effort for her not to snatch the clipboard from his hands and toss it on the ground then and there to make him look at her. She settled for spinning around and slamming the door shut. "I can't believe you did that," she hissed once she had his attention.

"Did what?"

"Forced your employees to be my friends. Who do you think you are?"

"Their boss," he replied, sharply, eyes flashing. "And I did not force anyone. I told them to treat you with respect, something I thought you were sorely in need of at the time. Or don't you remember how upset you were on that first day? When you told me about the trial?"

And broke down in his arms. "I remember," she said. All too well. Like so many times, Nico had been the rock she so desperately needed.

"That doesn't entitle you to go around speaking on my behalf." Hearing the complaint aloud, it sounded a lot less egregious than it had when she came marching down here. Still, she pressed on. There was some merit to her grievance. "I needed to win people over on my own, not because of your influence."

"And you did," Nico replied. She rolled her eyes. "Look, I simply told people to give you a chance. That if they got to know you, they would see that what the newspapers were saying was nothing but a load of garbage."

Exactly what Mario said.

"I assure you, *bella mia*, any goodwill you received you earned on your own." With a duck of his head, he offered a small smile. "You are irresistible, you know."

In spite her annoyance, Louisa's stomach gave

a little wobble. He wasn't getting off that easily, though. "Regardless, you should have told me what you were planning. I don't like the idea of everyone talking behind my back."

"They were already talking; I wanted to make sure they talked correctly. Besides, if I had mentioned my plans, you would have told me not to, making your job twice as hard."

He had a point, even if the logic didn't sit completely well with her.

"What else did you tell them?" she asked.

"Nothing. I swear."

She believed him. Knowing she could verify whatever he said, he had no reason not to answer truthfully.

His index finger hooked her chin. "My only intention was to make sure people treated you fairly," he said, thumbing her lower lip. "When you told me how badly your 'friends' treated you in Boston, I… I swore I wouldn't let you suffer like that again. I just wanted to erase the hurt from your eyes."

He gazed at her from beneath lowered lids, the black of his eyes obscured by thick dark lashes. Louisa found herself lost in them anyway. He had the power to distract her with a single touch, no matter how slight. Being with Nico was unlike anything she'd ever experienced. Not with Steven or any other man. It was as if she'd been stuck in darkness her entire life and had finally stepped into the light. Nico made her feel beautiful and smart and special and a thousand other adjectives she couldn't name. The sensation scared her to death.

And yet she couldn't stop herself.

"I hate seeing you sad," he whispered. "All I want is to make sure you are happy. I'm sorry if I overstepped."

"Your heart was in the right place."

"It was." He wanted to help her by encouraging her coworkers to get to know her. A far cry from trying to isolate her, the way Steven had done.

"Then I suppose I can forgive you. This time."

Smiling, Nico leaned in to kiss her. *"Grazie, bella mia."*

Oh, but she was so weak, Louisa thought to herself. One brush of Nico's lips, and she was ready to forgive everything. Forgot everything. He could betray her a thousand times and with one touch, she'd be his again. Heart and soul. The thought would terrify her, if Nico hadn't started kissing the patch of skin right below her jaw, obliterating all coherent thought.

From the way the clipboard just slipped from Nico's grasp, she wasn't the only one about to lose control. "What have you done to me, *bella mia*?" he whispered.

Precisely the question Louisa was asking herself. But then Nico kissed her deep, and she was swept away.

* * *

"Absolutely not," Louisa said, shaking her index finger. "I'm not letting you talk me out of it again."

Oh, but the spark in her eyes said he was welcome to try. They were discussing Louisa's moving back to the palazzo. The past two nights, Nico had managed to convince her she should postpone her departure. Not that she needed too much convincing.

Tonight, however, Louisa insisted she was sleeping in her own bed.

"Fine," he told her.

"Really?" Nico chuckled at how high her brows rose. She'd been expecting an argument. After all, as they'd both discovered, the persuasion was half the fun.

"Sure. You may sleep wherever you like. Of course," he said, trailing a finger down the back of her neck, "you won't be sleeping alone."

She made a soft strangled sound in her throat that made him want to kiss her all over. He loved how easily she responded to his suggestion and how she stubbornly fought to keep him from knowing. Her eyes would flutter shut and she would bite her lower lip. Inevitably her reaction would leak out anyway, and then he would be the one fighting to hide how she affected him. Surely, she knew how crazy she made him. He would give her the world on a silver platter if she asked.

So if she wanted to go back to the palazzo, to the palazzo they would go. The only reason he kept persuading her to stay was because he didn't want to spend a night without her.

Frightening how much he needed her. Frightening and exhilarating. Was this how his brother and sister felt when they fell in love? Or his parents? If so, perhaps he finally understood them a little bit better.

Although he would never throw a plate at Louisa. Of that he was certain.

"You never told me what you thought of dinner," he said, slipping an arm around her shoulder. The two of them had played guinea pig for Rafe's fall menu.

"It was delicious," she replied. "I've never had rabbit before. And don't try to change the subject."

"*Bistecca alla fiorentina* is a Tuscan specialty. And I'm not changing the subject. I already agreed to let you win."

"Let me, huh?" She reached up and entwined her fingers with the ones on her shoulder, a move that brought her face into perfect kissing proximity. Nico had no choice but to brush his lips across hers.

"Always,' he murmured.

"Except when you don't. Like the past two nights."

Recalling how they'd spent those two nights, Nico felt a satisfied groan rise in his throat. "I like to think we both won those arguments," he replied.

It was early still; the stars had yet to appear in the sky. Nevertheless, the fountain spotlights were already on. The brightness bounced off the coins scattered in the basin.

Reaching into the water, he picked up the first coin he saw and held it up. "A halfpenny for your thoughts," he said.

She laughed. "I was thinking about how much things have changed since I arrived in Monte Calanetti."

"Good changes, I hope."

"Some very good ones," she replied.

She looked so lovely, with the light framing her face. An angel to rival the nymph of the fountain. All those people tossing money and making wishes. He already had his wish standing before him. A fierce ache spread from the center of Nico's chest, giving birth to emotions that begged to be released. "I love you," he told her, the words bursting out of him in a rush.

Louisa's heart jumped to her throat. Of all the things he could have said, why did he have to say those three words?

"Nico—"

"I know," he rushed on, "it's too soon. It's too fast. Too... Too many things, but then again, it's not." His hand trembled as he stroked her cheek. "I think I have loved you for a very long time. Since long before the wedding."

Louisa wasn't sure if she wanted to run or cry. He was right; it was too soon. If she said the words back, it would mean accepting the fact she had once again fallen in love without thinking things through.

Even if it was already true.

That he seemed to know what she was thinking made the panic worse. "It's all right," he said, pressing his fingers to her lips. "I understand if you're not ready to say the words back. I just needed to tell you."

She was about to tell him she needed time—a lot more time—when a voice interrupted from behind them. "Nico! I thought that was you."

A wiry man with slick black hair approached them with a smile. "And Signorina Harrison. How lucky that I should run into you. Saves me the trouble of tracking you down by phone."

"Me?" She looked at Nico for help.

"I'm sorry, I should have introduced myself. I'm Dominic Merloni."

"From the bank?" Apparently he'd decided she was worth talking to after all.

If the banker noticed the chill in her voice, he was unfazed. "Yes, I wanted to apologize for canceling our meeting so abruptly the other day. There was a family emergency that took me out of town."

"How terrible," she said, not sure she believed him. "I hope everything's okay now."

"Better than ever, thank you. Anyway, since I didn't know when I would be returning, I told my secretary not to reschedule anything. Now that I'm back, I'm looking forward to sitting down and hearing more about your project. You are still thinking of turning the palazzo into a boutique hotel, are you not?"

"Yes! Definitely."

"Wonderful. Call my office tomorrow and we'll pick a time."

This was unbelievable. Here she'd convinced herself that her plans would need to wait another couple of years.

"Um…" She still didn't want to get her hopes up yet. Signor Merloni might be willing to listen, but that didn't erase her weak credit history. "I think before we meet, you should probably know that I'm recently divorced. My personal credit history is relatively new."

"Oh, I don't think that will be a problem," the banker said. "I'm sure you'll be a solid risk." His gaze darted to Nico as he spoke.

She should have known it was too good to be true.

"Well, it looks like we have occasion to celebrate," the winemaker said as they watched him walk away.

"Really?" she asked, narrowing her eyes. Whatever elation she was feeling had vanished, wiped out when the banker had tipped Nico's hand. "And what exactly do you want to celebrate? The fact that you talked Dominic into meeting with me or the fact you're a controlling jerk?"

As she hurled the words at him, Nico stiffened. "Louisa…"

"Don't try to deny it," she said. "I saw Dominic looking at you. He was about as subtle as an elephant. The guy might as well have come out and said you were backing the loan."

"I'm not backing anything."

He also wasn't denying his involvement. "You did talk with him, though."

"I told him I thought the project had potential."

The Amatucci seal of approval. Which, as everyone in Monte Calanetti knew, was as good as a guarantee. Louisa could tear her hair out. No, correction. She could tear Nico's hair out. Every curly strand.

"I can't believe you," she said, shaking her head.

"I don't understand. What did I do that's so terrible?"

What did he do? "You went behind my back, that's what."

"I was trying to help you."

"Funny, I don't recall asking for it. In fact, *I specifically asked you not to help.*" Turning on her heel, she marched to the bench but was too aggravated to sit down.

Nico marched up behind her.

"What was I supposed to do?" he asked. "You were putting your plans on hold because of the man. Was I supposed to stand back and let your dreams fall apart even though I have the ability to stop it?"

"Yes!" she hissed as she spun around to face him. "That's exactly what you should have done."

"You're kidding."

"No, I'm not. It wasn't your dream to save. It was mine."

"But you weren't doing anything. To save it."

"And that's my decision to make, too. I don't need you coming in and taking over."

"Taking over?" He looked stunned, as though someone had told him pigs could fly. "What are you talking about?"

He was kidding, right? They were arguing about his influencing a banker on her behalf and he was asking her to explain herself?

Then again, maybe he didn't understand. Taking over was so ingrained in men like him, they didn't know how not to be in control.

Louisa shook her head. When she'd found out about that damn staff meeting, she should have realized then, but she'd let him sweep her concerns away. Same as she did whenever she talked about going back to the palazzo. He need only touch her and poof! Her arguments disappeared.

Because nothing felt as safe and perfect as being in his arms.

"All I wanted was to help," Nico continued. "I thought it would make you happy."

"Well, it didn't," she said, sitting down. Kind of ironic they would be arguing about this in the same spot where they'd kissed a few days earlier. The harvest festival had been one of the most magical days of her life.

How much of those memories were real? "What else have you influenced without my knowing?" she asked. "Oh my God, the baptism. Did you ask your sister to make me Rosabella's godmother?"

"No. Of course not. No one tells Marianna what to do. You know that."

"Maybe. I don't know what to believe anymore." Other than knowing she'd created some of the problem herself, that is. Leaning on Nico came too easily. His strength made her feel too safe. What was it she'd said the day of the festival? *You'd rescue me.* From the moment the news about Luscious Louisa broke, she'd come to rely on him to catch her when she fell.

"I'll tell you what you can believe," Nico said. He was kneeling in front of her, holding her hands, his eyes imploring her to let him catch her one more time. "You can believe that I would never try to hurt you. I love you."

"I know." If only he realized, his saying he loved her only made things worse.

Suddenly, she understood why she'd been so frightened when he'd said those words earlier. Deep inside she knew that if she accepted his love, then she would have to acknowledge the feelings in her own heart. Nico was already her greatest weakness. Once she admitted her feelings, she'd lose what little power she had left. Before she knew it, she would be swallowed alive again. "I promised myself that would never happen again."

"What would never happen again?" he asked.

She hadn't realized she'd spoken aloud. Since she had, however, she might as well see her thoughts through. "I swore I would never let anyone control my life again," she told him.

"Control? What the…?" Nico sat back on his heels. "I'm not trying to control you."

"Maybe not on purpose," she replied. No, definitely not on purpose. "You just can't help yourself."

Same way she wouldn't be able to help herself from letting him.

"Goodbye, Nico." She pulled her hands free. "I'll pick up my things later on."

"I'm not Steven."

She was ten feet away when he spoke. The comment was soft, barely loud enough for her to hear.

Turning, she saw Nico on his feet, hands balled into fists by his side. "I'm not Steven," he repeated, this time a little louder.

"I never said you were."

"Then stop running from me like I am!"

Didn't he get it? She wasn't running from just him. She was running from herself, too.

CHAPTER TWELVE

NICO STARED AT the vine-covered wall. Once upon a time, climbing to the other side meant escaping the turmoil that engulfed his house and finding tranquility. Too bad that wasn't possible anymore. Only thing crossing the wall would do today was make the pain in his chest more acute. Either because he didn't see Louisa or because he did, and she pushed him away again.

He was still trying to comprehend what had happened the other night. One moment he was declaring his love, the next... How had everything gone so horribly wrong?

"Signor?"

He forgot that Mario was waiting for an answer. They were scheduled to harvest the fields at the palazzo today. The final field of the season, Nico always saved it for last because the grapes took the longest to ripen. Mario wanted to know if he planned to check on the workers' progress. Thus the quandary over crossing the wall.

"You go ahead," he decided. "You can supervise on your own."

The young man straightened. "If you think so."

"I do." No need for the student to know that Nico was a coward, and that was why he didn't want to visit.

Besides, there was someone else he needed to speak with.

Marianna answered the door in a long floral dress, looking uncharacteristically tousled and unmade-up. Holding Rosabella on her right shoulder, she looked him up and down. "You look worse than I do," she remarked, "and I haven't had a good night's sleep in days. What's the matter?"

"I think I might have messed up," he replied.

"Messed up how?"

"With Louisa." As briefly as he could, he explained what had happened a few nights earlier, including what happened with Dominic.

"Tell me you didn't," she said when he finished.

"I was trying to help," he said. Why did everyone have a problem with him talking to the banker? "I gave my recommendation, same as I would for Rafe, or Ryan, for that matter."

"But we aren't talking about Rafe or Ryan—although it's nice to know you would speak on my husband's behalf—we're talking about Louisa. A woman who found out her husband had been lying to her about everything. And you went behind her back. Twice!"

"To help," Nico reminded her. "Steven Clark was a thief."

"Yes, I know, but surely you can see how keeping a secret, even a well-meaning one, would feel like a betrayal to her?"

Yes, he could.

"You owe her a very large apology," Marianna told him.

"If only the solution was that simple."

"You mean there's more?" The baby started to squirm, and she switched shoulders. "What else did you do?"

"Not me—her ex-husband."

"What did he do? Besides steal from all those people?"

Nico ran a hand through his curls. He'd already said too much. Having already broken Louisa's faith, he didn't dare break it further. "Let's just say he believed in holding the people he loved as close as possible."

"Oh. I think I understand."

"You do?"

"I think so. And if I'm right, then yes, you've messed up very badly."

"She accused me of trying to take over her life. I wasn't," he added when Marianna arched a brow.

"Not intentionally anyway," she murmured.

"Louisa said the same thing."

That his sister laughed hurt. "Poor Nico," she said, using her free hand to pat his knee. "It's not your fault. It's your nature to want to rush in and take over. You tried to with Ryan and me when I was pregnant."

"Great. So now you're saying I tried to control your life, as well."

"Don't be silly. I'm used to you. I learned a long time ago to ignore you when you start giving orders I don't feel like obeying. But I'm not someone like Louisa who is struggling to rebuild her life. I can imagine your interference would make her feel very powerless. Especially since you kept your actions secret. Why didn't you tell her?"

"Because I…" Because he knew she would tell him no. "I was trying to help," he finished, as if his intentions excused his actions. "I wouldn't have talked to Dominic if I didn't have faith in her."

"I know you wouldn't, but can you see how someone in Louisa's position might see things differently?"

Yes, he could. Especially someone who'd spent so many years trapped in a controlling relationship. Nico washed a hand over his face. So focused had he been on making Louisa happy, he'd let his desires blind him to what she truly needed. "I'm no better than her ex-husband, am I?"

"Your heart was in the right place."

Small comfort when life blows up in your face. He'd trade his good intentions for having Louisa back in a second.

At that moment, Rosabella started to squirm again, wriggling her tiny torso against Marianna's body. "I swear," his sister said, as she tried to make the baby comfortable, "this little one is part eel. Spends half her day squirming. Don't you, Rosabella?" She nuzzled the baby's curls. "You know what, why don't you hold her for a few minutes? Maybe Uncle Nico is what she needs to settle down."

Doubtful. He could barely keep *himself* calm at the moment. "Marianna, I don't think—" Too late. She deposited his niece in his waiting arms and he found himself looking into Rosa's big brown eyes. For the second time in his life, Nico's heart lurched.

"She's so little," he said, risking a finger stroke against Rosa's cheek. The baby responded with a sleepy blink.

"She likes you," Marianna murmured.

"Louisa said I'd fall in love," he whispered.

"Excuse me?"

"When we were talking about being godparents. She told me I would fall in love with Rosa."

He remembered every detail of their conversation, from the advice she gave to the way the sun crowned her head as he said goodbye. "She was right in more ways than one."

His heart threatened to crack open, the way it had every hour since Louisa had said goodbye. Struggling to keep the pieces together, he looked to his sister. "I love her," he said in a quiet voice.

"I know."

Neither of them had to say what they were both thinking. That finally after years without it, Nico had found love, only to chase it away.

"I tried to explain myself the other night but she wouldn't listen, and now she won't take my phone calls," he said. "I'd go to the palazzo, but I'm afraid she'll refuse to come out." Or send him away. Either outcome frightened him into inertia. "Tell me, Marianna. What do I do?"

"I don't think you're going to like my answer."

"If you're going to tell me there's nothing I can do, you're right. There has to be something I can do." Surely she didn't expect him to sit around and do nothing while the love of his life slipped through his fingers. "If I could only get her to talk with me."

"Why? So you can explain and try to charm her into forgiving you?"

Nico held his sleeping niece a little closer. "Is that such a bad plan?"

"I don't know. How well did charm work for her ex-husband?"

"I'm not him."

"Then prove it to her."

"How? How do I make her see that I don't want to control her?"

"You let her be her own person. And that includes letting her come to you for help when she's ready.

"What if she never comes to me again?"

He didn't realize his knee was bouncing in agitation until Marianna put her hand on his leg. "Poor Nico. So used to being in charge of the situation. Haven't you figured out by now that love isn't something that makes sense? If it did, our parents would never have gotten together."

Their parents. Despite his sadness, he had to smile at her comment. "Never were two people less suited for one another," he said.

"Or more meant to be," Marianna replied, squeezing his knee. "I think you and Louisa are meant to be, as well, but you have to be patient."

"I don't know if I can." Each day that passed without speaking to her made the hole in his chest a little wider.

"Of course you can, Mr. Viticulture. Think of it like a harvest. You wouldn't pick a grape with a poor Brix level, would you?"

"No," he replied. "But waiting on a grape is a lot less painful, too."

"You can do it."

He smiled at the woman beside him. His beautiful baby sister all grown-up and glowing with motherhood. "When did you get so wise?"

"Oh, I've always been wise. You just never bothered to ask me for advice. Might as well face it, dear brother," she said, "when it comes to love, you've got a lot to learn."

Yes, he did. He only hoped he'd be able to learn with Louisa by his side.

If space was what she needed to find her way back to him, then space was what he would give her.

His resolve lasted five minutes. Then the phone rang.

"After weeks of speculation, the Halencian royal family confirmed today that Prince Antonio and Princess Christina are expecting their first child. The royal heir is due to arrive early next spring. No other details have been released..."

The television screen showed a photo of Antonio and Christina dancing at their wedding. The same photo that had reignited the Luscious Louisa scandal. Nice to know news outlets recycled resources.

Clicking off the news, Louisa tossed the remote onto the cushions. She was happy for the royal couple. Really she was. They may have had some bumpy times at the beginning of their marriage, but the pair were very much in love.

Funny how that had happened to a lot of the people she knew in Monte Calanetti. The whole "love conquering all" thing, that is. Too bad it missed her. Then again, maybe it was her fault. After all, she'd loved Steven and love hadn't come in to conquer anything. What made her think the situation would be any different simply because she loved—

Oh God, was she really ready to admit she loved Nico?

She checked her phone for messages. What was a little salt in the wound when you were already miserable, right? Nothing. After six impassioned voice mails, Nico had stopped calling. Guess he'd finally gotten the message. Or lost interest.

Make up your mind, Louisa. What do you want?

Nico, a voice whispered. She shut the voice off. What she wanted was to stop feeling as if she'd been kicked in the chest. Nothing she did seemed to curb the ache. Every day she immersed herself in cleaning and home renovations, working herself to the point of exhaustion. There wasn't a piece of wood she hadn't polished or a weed she hadn't removed from the back garden. But despite collapsing in a deep sleep every night, she woke in the morning feeling the same emptiness inside.

The doorbell rang. "Go away," she called to whoever was on the other side.

"Louisa!" Nico bellowed from the other side of the door. "Open up. I need to talk to you."

Careful what you wish for. The anger in his voice could mean only one thing. He'd found out about the Realtor.

He pounded on the door again. "Louisa! You let me in this minute or so help me I will kick the door in."

Nothing like a threat to kill her self-pity. Anger took over and she reached for the doorknob. "If you damage so much as a speck of dust, I'll…"

Dear Lord, he looked awful. One of the qualities she'd noticed from the beginning was Nico's robust appearance. The man on her doorstep looked tired, his healthy color turned pale and sallow. His eyes, while flashing with anger, were flat and lifeless beneath the spark. He looked, to be blunt, as bad as she felt.

"Is it true?" Without waiting for an invitation or answer, he stomped inside, toward the main staircase. There he stood at the foot, arms folded across his body, waiting.

"Tell me you're not seriously thinking of selling your home."

"You got the call, didn't you?"

"But why?" he asked.

"Seriously, you have to ask?" He and Monte Calanetti were irrevocably entwined. How was she supposed to stay in the village and live her life when every corner she turned would present some reminder of him?

"I thought it would make things easier," she told him, walking into the living room. Maybe if she dismissed him…

Of course he followed. "For who?" he asked. "You?"

"Yes." And for him. He wouldn't be forced to share his hometown with an ex-lover as his neighbor.

Nico didn't say a word. Instead he crossed the room, to the cabinet where she stored the fernet. At first she thought he might pour himself a glass, but he put the bottle back on the shelf.

"Amazing," he said, shaking his head. "You do like to run away from your problems, don't you?"

"Excuse me?"

"Well, you ran away from Boston to Monte Calanetti. You wanted to run away when the paparazzi came and now you are running away from me."

Louisa couldn't believe him. "I'm not running from you," she said.

"Oh really? Then what are you doing?"

"I'm..." She was...

Starting fresh again. In a new place. Away from Monte Calanetti.

All right, maybe she was running away. Maybe she needed to run away in order to save her independence. "What I do or don't do is none of your business," she snapped. "If I want to sell the palazzo, I will."

"Is that so? And here I thought I exercised such control over your actions."

Damn him. Who did he think he was, twisting

her words? "If I am leaving Monte Calanetti, it's because you tried to take over my life, and you know it."

"I did no such thing."

"Oh yeah? Then what was calling Dominic?"

"A mistake."

A damn big one, too. She was tired of having this argument. As far as she was concerned, they'd already had it one too many times.

Unfortunately, Nico thought differently. "It was wrong of me to call Dominic without telling you. I was excited to be able to help you, and I didn't think about how my help might make you feel."

Louisa had liked the conversation better before. Anger was so much easier to oppose than this softer, conciliatory tone.

She stared out the window. The Tuscan hills were starting to turn. Shades of brown mixed with the green. In another few months, it would be a year since her arrival. Seemed like only yesterday she and Dani had met on the bus from Florence. And she remembered the first time she'd met Nico. He'd sauntered through the front door without knocking and demanded proof she owned the palazzo. *Here's a man who insists on being in charge*, she remembered thinking. Her insides had practically melted at the thought, and that had scared the hell out of her. Because she didn't want to be attracted to a strong man.

"Scared," she said, her breath marking the glass.

"I don't understand." He replied.

"Your going to Dominic. It frightened me."

"I made you feel powerless."

She shook her head. "No. You made me feel like I'd met another Prince Charming. Actually, that's not true," she said, looking over her shoulder. "I already knew you were Prince Charming. Calling Dominic made it obvious."

"I still don't…"

No surprise. She probably wasn't making much sense. "I liked that you came to my rescue," she told him.

"And that scares you."

It terrified her. With a small shrug, she turned back to the hills. "I need to be my own person. When I'm with you, it's too easy to give in and let you run the show."

"Could have fooled me. In fact, I seem to recall more than one argument over my trying to run the show."

His shadow appeared in the window. Louisa could tell from the warmth buffeting her back, or rather the lack of it, that he was making a point of keeping his distance. "Do you know why Floriana and I didn't work?" he asked.

The odd shift in conversation confused her, but Louisa went along with it. "No. Why?"

"Because she was too perfect. I realized that just now."

"If this is supposed to make me feel better…"

"Wait, hear me out," he said. "Floriana… She and I never argued. She was always logical, always agreeable, always in tune with my thinking."

"She was perfect." While Louisa was the imperfect American who ran away from her problems. Both descriptions sickened her. "I get it."

"I don't think you do" was Nico's reply. The warmth from his body moved a step closer. Not too much, but enough so Louisa could better feel its presence. "Floriana might have been perfect, but she wasn't perfect for me. That was why I couldn't truly love her. Do you understand?"

She was afraid to.

"I need a woman who challenges me every single day," he said. "Someone who is smart and beautiful, and who is not afraid to put me in my place when I overstep."

"You make it sound simple."

"On the contrary, I think it might be very hard. I don't know for sure. I've never been in love until you."

Until her. The declaration washed over her, powerful in its simplicity. Nico Amatucci loved her. And she… Panic clamped down on the thought like a vise.

"I know you are afraid," he said when she let out

a choked sob. The anguish in his voice told her how much he was struggling between wanting to close the distance and respecting her need for space.

"I know that Steven left you with some very deep scars and that you are afraid of making the same mistakes. I am not Steven, though. Please know that no matter what happens between us, I will always want you to be your own person.

"So," she heard him say, "if you want to run away, that's your choice. All I ask is that you don't use me as your excuse." There were a lot of things Louisa wanted to say in response, but when she opened her mouth to speak, the words died on her tongue. In the end, she stayed where she was, afraid to turn to look lest she break down when she saw Nico's face. She heard his footsteps on the tile, the click of the front door, and then she was alone.

She'd said she wanted to stand on her own two feet. She also wanted Nico's arms around her. Desperately. What did that say about her?

That you love him. The words she'd been fighting to keep buried broke free and echoed loud in her heart. No amount of running away or lying to herself would make them disappear. She loved Nico Amatucci. She was *in* love with Nico Amatucci.

Now what? With a sob, she sank to the floor. Did she continue with her plans? Move again and spend her life being haunted by two past mistakes?

Or did she stay in the village she'd come to think

of as home and somehow find the courage to let her love for Nico grow?

Wiping her eyes, she looked out once more at the Tuscan hillside and the vineyards that stretched out before her. How much she'd come to love this view. And this palazzo.

She looked around at her surroundings. A lot had changed around here in nine months. If her ancestors could see this place now, they wouldn't recognize their old home. It wasn't the same crumbling building she'd found when she'd arrived.

Maybe she wasn't the same woman either. She certainly wasn't the impressionable young girl who'd fallen in love with Steven Clark. She'd loved, lost, withstood public scorn and found a new home. *You're a lot stronger than you give yourself credit for,* Nico had once said. Maybe it was time to start giving herself credit. Time to believe she *was* strong.

Maybe even strong enough to fall in love with a strong man.

"I asked Lindsay Sullivan if she would stop by the meeting, as well. It might be useful to get a professional event planner's input, even if she does specialize in weddings. Is that all right with you, Nico?"

"A wedding planner is fine," Nico replied. "Whatever you want to do."

"Whatever I...? All right," Rafe said, plopping down on the other side of the table. "What have you done with the real Nico Amatucci? Usually by now you would have rearranged the agenda items and brainstormed three or four new ones. Instead, you've hardly said a word. What gives?" Folding his arms, the chef tipped back in his chair and waited.

No doubt he found Nico's shrug an unsatisfactory response. "It's your committee."

"That I started with the full knowledge that you would take over. Honestly, I wouldn't have gone to all this trouble if I didn't think you would do the bulk of the heavy lifting."

"Sorry to disappoint you," he replied.

"Leave him alone, Rafe. He's nursing a broken heart." Walking past, Dani gave her husband a playful smack on the back of the head. "Remember how depressed you were when I left Monte Calanetti?"

"Depressed is a little strong. Ow!" He rubbed the back of his head. "I was joking. I was also trying to distract him from his problems."

"News flash. The playful banter isn't helping." Each quip was like salt in his already raw wounds.

"We're sorry," Dani said, taking a seat.

"No, I'm sorry," he quickly replied. "You shouldn't have to censor your happiness for my sake." Then, because he was clearly a glutton for punishment, he added, "I don't suppose you've heard anything?"

She shook her head. "Nothing. I called a couple

of times, but she isn't picking up her phone. She's still in town, though."

"I know." He saw the lights on in the palazzo. Yesterday, while in the vines, he thought he caught a glimpse of her on the balcony, and he almost climbed up to join her. But since he was practicing patience, like his sister suggested, he stayed away.

"Do you think she'll go through with selling the palazzo?" Rafe asked.

God, but Nico hoped not. "It's up to her." He personally hadn't returned the Realtor's call. Probably should or else risk losing the property altogether. The idea of someone—anyone—other than Louisa living next door... Grabbing a fork, he stabbed at a *cornetto*. Far preferable to stabbing anything else. "It's her decision to make," he repeated, as much to remind himself as anything.

"Whose decision to make what?" a beautifully familiar voice asked. Nico looked up in time to see Louisa walking into the main dining room. She was dressed in a navy blue suit, the kind a banker might wear. The dark material made her hair appear more white than ever. Perhaps that was why she was wearing it pulled back in a clip. This, he realized with a jolt, was a different Louisa than the woman he'd left the other day. The woman before him carried herself with confidence and grace.

"Sorry I'm late," she said, setting a leather portfolio on the table. "Oh, please tell me that carafe is American coffee."

"Espresso," Rafe replied. He sounded as astounded as Nico felt. A quick look at Dani said she shared the feeling, as well.

Fortunately for all of them, Dani didn't have a problem saying something aloud.

"We didn't think you were coming," she said.

Pink appeared in her cheeks. "I wasn't sure I was going to attend either. I didn't make up my mind until last night."

"And the suit?"

"Confidence booster," she said, reaching for the plate of pastries that was in the center of the table. "I have a business meeting after this one."

"You do?" Nico sat up straighter. This was what he feared. She'd come to say goodbye. "You found someone to buy the palazzo?"

"No, someone to help me turn it into a hotel." Her blue eyes found his. "It appears I'm not leaving Monte Calanetti after all."

"You're not?" For a second, he was afraid he'd heard her wrong. There was a smile in her eyes, though. Would she be smiling if she was about to break his heart?

The rest of the restaurant faded into the background. Nico was vaguely aware of Rafe and Dani excusing themselves from the room, not that it mattered. He only had eyes for the woman in front of him. Everything else was background noise.

"What made you change your mind?" he asked.

Of course, her staying didn't mean she wanted him back in her life. He tried to remind himself not to get his hopes up. She'd never even said she loved him.

But she was smiling. They both were.

"For starters? A good long look at where I was." Her lip trembled, breaking the spell between them. She looked down at her pastry. "I realized I'd been stuck in the past. Not so much regarding what happened— although I was stuck about those things, too—but more like frozen in time. In my head, I saw myself as that same impressionable twenty-one-year-old girl. I forgot how much time had passed.'

Afraid she was about to beat herself up, he cut in. "Not so much time."

"Enough that I should know better," she told him.

She wasn't making sense. Confused, he waited as she got up from the table. Her high heels tapped out her paces on the terra-cotta.

"I should have known that the person I am today isn't the same as the person I was back then. At least I shouldn't be, if I let myself grow up.

"I'm not making much sense, am I?" she said, looking at him.

"No."

"I was afraid of that." Her small smile quickly

faded away. "What I'm trying to say is that you were right. I was afraid of repeating the past. For so long I thought I was trapped in my marriage. Then the trial happened, and suddenly I had a second chance. Throughout the entire trial, I swore to myself I would never let myself become trapped again."

And along came Nico charging in to make everything better. Exactly what she didn't need. He'd heard enough. "It's all right, Louisa. I understand."

"No, you don't," she said, walking to him. "I should have realized that I can't make the same mistake, because I'm not the same person. I can make new mistakes, but I can't make the same ones."

Through her speech, Nico had been fighting the kernel of hope that wanted to take root in his chest. All of her rambling sounded suspiciously like it was leading to a declaration. Until he heard the words, however, he was too afraid to believe. "Are you saying…?"

"I'm saying I've fallen in love with you, Nico Amatucci. I started falling the day I arrived in Monte Calanetti, and I haven't stopped."

She loved him. "You know that I'm still going to want to rush in and fix things."

"And I'll probably get mad and accuse you of trying to take over."

"I'd expect no less."

The eyes that found his this time were shining

with moisture. "Because no one said love had to be perfect."

"Just perfect for us." After days of separation, Nico couldn't hold himself back a moment longer. Jumping to his feet, he rushed to take her in his arms. Immediately, he felt a hand against his chest.

"I still have scars," she said. "You're going to have to be patient with me."

"I'll wait for as long as it takes," he promised. "There's no rushing the harvest. A long story," he added when she frowned. "I'll tell you about it later. Right now, I'd much rather kiss you."

Her arms were around his neck before he finished the sentence. *"Bella mia,"* he whispered against her lips. *Thank you*, he prayed to himself. All his dreams, everything he'd ever wanted, he was holding in his arms right now. Nothing else mattered.

As his lips touched hers, one last thought flashed across his mind.

No sweeter wine...

EPILOGUE

February 14, Valentine's Day

IF YOU ASKED LOUISA, the palazzo had never looked lovelier, not even when the place had hosted the royal wedding party. Standing in the ballroom doorway, she couldn't stop smiling at the crowd of people who were there to celebrate the opening of her hotel.

This weekend, the palazzo would only host a handful of overnight guests, mostly friends who had agreed to be guinea pigs and test the service. They would open to the general public on a limited basis next weekend, and she hoped to be fully operational by summer.

The crowd was here for the first annual St. Valentine's Ball. Billed as an opportunity to experience medieval romance and pageantry, the idea was the tourist development committee's first official success.

A flash of red sequins caught her eye. "Lindsay's

outdone herself this time, hasn't she?" Marianna said, appearing by her side. "No wonder she does so many A-list weddings."

"No kidding." The room was a gorgeous display of roses and red tapestry. "We were lucky she offered to help, what with her schedule." But then, the woman had a soft spot for the village since it was where she'd met her husband. He was here with her tonight. A quick look across the dance floor found the two of them stealing a kiss in the corner. They were caught by Connor and Isabella, who'd apparently had a similar idea. Yet another couple who had found love here.

Monte Calanetti seemed to have a romantic effect on people.

"I overheard a couple talking in the lobby about booking a room for next year's ball," Marianna was saying. "I hope you're planning to take advanced reservations."

"Of course," Louisa replied. Talk about a foolish question. "My business partner would kill me if I didn't," Louisa replied. "Speaking of, where is your husband anyway?"

"He went upstairs to check on the baby and her nanny."

"Didn't you just check on them five minutes ago?"

"I did, but Ryan has to see for himself. Daddy's little girl, you know."

Louisa laughed. Sometimes she thought her two friends were competing to see who could dote on their daughter the most.

The idea of asking Marianna's husband, Ryan, to invest in her project had happened completely by accident. Literally. Louisa had almost knocked him over the day she had taken the palazzo off the market. As luck would have it, he'd been looking for a new start-up project. Neither Nico nor Marianna had any idea until the partnership was official.

Naturally, when he found out, Nico had teased her about going behind his back. In reality, he was excited for her. It was a sign of how good things were going between them that they could joke about that terrible night last fall.

A tap on her shoulder pulled her from her thoughts. "Nico told me to have you join him in the other room," Marianna said.

It never failed. As soon as she heard Nico's name, a shiver ran down Louisa's spine. The man would forever have that effect on her. "Did he say what he wanted?"

The brunette waved her hand. "You know my brother tells me nothing. I think he and Angelo are up to something. I saw them and Rafe with their heads together. Their poor, poor wives."

"You might want to include yourself in that category," Louisa reminded her. "Whatever they're up to, I'm sure it's only a matter of time before Ryan's involved, too."

"He'd better not be."

The two of them walked toward what was now the hotel lobby. Of all the changes that the palazzo was undergoing, this was the most drastic. What had been the plain entranceway was now a richly appointed lobby. Louisa had done her best to keep the structural changes to a minimum, although she did concede to installing a small built-in counter that served as both the front desk and concierge location.

The staircase remained the same, however. Richly polished, the stairs made a welcoming statement to everyone who walked in. It was in a group gathered around the bottom banister post that Louisa found her man. He was talking with his brother, Angelo, and Angelo's wife, Kayla, who had flown in from New York City. Rafe and Dani were also chatting.

Nico stepped to the side slightly, drawing her attention, and her heart stuttered. He sure could wear a tuxedo. Wasn't fair. Tomorrow he would be back in his T-shirt and jeans and would look just as sexy. Worse, she'd bet he would look just as good fifty years from now, while she'd probably end up with gray hair and a thickening waist.

So you think the two of you will be together in fifty years, do you? Nico caught her eye and winked.

Yeah, she decided. She did.

At her arrival, Nico leaned in and whispered something in Angelo's ear. His brother nodded. "There you are, *bella mia*!" he greeted. Wrapping his arms around her waist, he pulled her into a lingering kiss. Same as she did whenever Nico touched her, Louisa melted into his embrace. Such an overt public display of affection surprised her. She chalked it up to the champagne and the atmosphere.

"I missed you," Nico whispered before releasing her.

"Down, boy. This dress isn't made for manhandling." She smoothed the wrinkles from the pink chiffon skirt before whispering in return, "I missed you, too.

"Is that why you wanted to see me?" she asked. Not that she would ever turn down a kiss, but again, even for Nico, the behavior seemed extreme.

"The kiss was merely a bonus. I was looking for you because I have a surprise."

"For me?"

"No, for my brother, Angelo. Cover your eyes."

Louisa did what she was told and seconds later, she felt Nico's breath tickling her ear. "I wanted to do something to congratulate you for everything you've done with the palazzo. Carlos, he would be proud. I know I am."

Warmth filled her from head to toe. She didn't

need a surprise. Nico's respect meant everything. "Okay," he whispered. "Open them."

"Nico, I don't need— Mom?"

The silver-haired woman standing at the foot of the stairs offered her a watery smile. "Hello, Louisa."

"I—" She couldn't believe her mother was standing the lobby. "How—"

"Signor Amatucci flew me here. He wanted me to see what you've done. It's wonderful, sweetheart."

"Mom..." She couldn't finish the sentence. Instead, she ran and threw her arms around the woman, holding on to her as tightly as she could. "I missed you so much," she managed to choke out. Until this moment, she hadn't realized just how much. "I'm so sorry."

"No, sweetheart, I am. I let us grow apart, but I promise I won't let that happen again." Pulling away, her mother cupped her face like she used to do when Louisa was a little girl and had a bad dream. "Okay?"

Louisa nodded. This was the best surprise she could imagine. "Thank you," she said when Nico joined them.

"My pleasure," he replied before looking serious "You're not angry I went behind your back?"

"Are you kidding? No way." If anything, his kindness only made her love him more. A pretty amazing feat, since she already loved him more than seemed possible.

She saw the same love in Nico's eyes. "Good. Because a woman should always be able to share her engagement with her mother."

Her engagement? A warm frisson passed through her at the words. She'd be lying if the idea of spending the rest of her life with Nico hadn't crossed her mind during these past few months. Trying to imagine life without him was... Well, it was like staring at a blank wall.

Still, she wasn't about to let him know that. The man needed to be kept on his toes, after all. Arms folded, she lifted her chin and said in her most haughty voice, "There you go, taking charge again. What makes you think we're getting married?"

"A man can hope, can't he?" Nico said, reaching into his pocket. Louisa gasped when she saw the small velvet box.

Bending on one knee, he held it out to her with a shaking hand. "Louisa Harrison, my beautiful, haughty American princess, you are the only woman I will ever love. Will you marry me?"

There was only one answer she could give. Same as there could only be one man she would ever want to be with forever. "Yes," she breathed. "Yes, I will marry you, Nico Amatucci."

He pulled her into another kiss, and this time Louisa didn't care how wrinkled her dress got. As his lips slanted over hers and the crowd burst into applause, she felt the last ghosts of her life with Steven disappear forever. She'd found a new life, a new home, a new love, here, in the vineyards of Monte Calanetti.

And they were better than she'd ever dreamed possible.

* * * * *

COMING NEXT MONTH FROM
ⓗ HARLEQUIN®
Romance

Available March 8, 2016

#4511 THE GREEK'S READY-MADE WIFE
Brides for the Greek Tycoons
by Jennifer Faye
Tycoon Cristo needs to marry to secure a vital deal and believes that
chambermaid Kyra Pappas will make the perfect convenient bride. But
relationships have only ever meant heartache for these two lost hearts—
together can they make their fairy-tale ending finally come true...?

#4512 CROWN PRINCE'S CHOSEN BRIDE
by Kandy Shepherd
Chef Gemma knows forever isn't possible with duty-bound Tristan—no
matter how charming this crown prince is! But when Tristan throws out
the royal rule book, all it takes is two little words for Gemma to get her
happy-ever-after..."I do!"

#4513 BILLIONAIRE, BOSS...BRIDEGROOM?
Billionaires of London
by Kate Hardy
CEO Hugh has one rule: he never mixes business with pleasure! Until he
needs a fake date and decides his quirky new graphic designer, Bella,
is the perfect candidate. With Bella by his
side, Hugh realizes that some rules are worth
breaking, especially if it means forever with
Bella. So, down on one knee, he'll prove it!

#4514 MARRIED FOR THEIR
MIRACLE BABY
by Soraya Lane
Ballerina Saffron is swept off her feet by
tycoon Blake Goldsmith—but she doesn't
expect his proposal of a convenient marriage!
Blake promises to help her fulfill her dancing
dreams, except another dream comes true...
she's pregnant! So what will this mean for
their fake marriage?

**YOU CAN FIND MORE INFORMATION
ON UPCOMING HARLEQUIN® TITLES,
FREE EXCERPTS AND MORE AT
WWW.HARLEQUIN.COM.**

HRLPCNM0216

LARGER-PRINT BOOKS!
GET 2 FREE LARGER-PRINT NOVELS PLUS
2 FREE GIFTS!

HARLEQUIN®

Romance

From the Heart, For the Heart

*The last thing chambermaid Kyra Pappas expects
when she enters Cristo Kiriakis's hotel suite is a
proposal! But is a marriage of convenience
enough for romantic Kyra?*

*Read on for a sneak preview of
THE GREEK'S READY-MADE WIFE,
the first in **Jennifer Faye**'s spell-binding duet
BRIDES FOR THE GREEK TYCOONS.*

It wasn't until the waiter had placed the cupcake in front
of her that she realized there was a diamond ring sitting
atop the large dollop of frosting. The jewel was big. No,
it was huge.

Kyra gasped.

The waiter immediately backed away. Cristo moved
from his chair and retrieved the ring. What was he up to?
Was it a mistake that he was going to correct? Because no
one purchased a ring that big for someone who was just
their fake fiancée.

Cristo dropped to his knee next to her chair. Her mouth
opened but no words came out. Was he going to propose
to her? Right here? In front of everyone?

Cristo gazed into her eyes. "Kyra, you stumbled into
my life, reminding me of all that I'd been missing. You
showed me that there's more to life than business. You
make me smile. You make me laugh. I can only hope to

make you nearly as happy. Will you make me the happiest man in the world and marry me?"

The words were perfect. The sentiment was everything a woman could hope for. She knew this was where she was supposed to say *yes*, but even though her jaw moved, the words were trapped in her throat. Instead, she nodded and blinked back the involuntary rush of emotions. Someday she hoped the right guy would say those words to her and mean them.

Her eyelids fluttered closed. His smooth lips pressed to hers. He was delicious, tasting sweet like the bottle of bubbly he'd insisted on ordering. She'd thought it'd just been to celebrate their business arrangement. She had no idea it was part of this seductive proposal. This man was as dangerous to her common sense as he was delicious enough to kiss all night long.

When applause and whistles filled the restaurant, it shattered the illusion. Kyra crashed back to earth and reluctantly pulled back. Her gaze met his passion-filled eyes. He wanted her. That part couldn't be faked. So that kiss had been more than a means to prove to the world that their relationship was real. The kiss had been the heart-pounding, soul-stirring genuine article.

Don't miss
THE GREEK'S READY-MADE WIFE
by Jennifer Faye,
available March 2016 wherever
Harlequin® Romance
books and ebooks are sold.

www.Harlequin.com

THE WORLD IS BETTER WITH *Romance*

Harlequin has everything from contemporary, passionate and heartwarming to suspenseful and inspirational stories.

Whatever your mood, we have a romance just for you!

Connect with us to find your next great read, special offers and more.

f /HarlequinBooks

🐦 @HarlequinBooks

www.HarlequinBlog.com

www.Harlequin.com/Newsletters

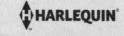

ℍ HARLEQUIN®

A *Romance* FOR EVERY MOOD™

www.Harlequin.com